● 現代英米児童文学評伝叢書 2 ●

谷本誠剛／原　昌／三宅興子／吉田新一 編

L.M. Montgomery

● 桂　宥子 ●

KTC中央出版

現代英米児童文学評伝叢書 2

目 次

L.M. Montgomery

I その生涯──人と作品── ……… 3

はじめに ……… 4
モンゴメリの日記／
モンゴメリの故郷──プリンス・エドワード島

1．子ども時代 ……… 12
誕生／母との死別／祖父母との生活／
孤独な少女時代──空想の世界への逃避／読書の喜び／
書く喜び／作家になる決心

2．10代のビッグ・イベント ……… 21
西部への旅／西部で出会った忘れがたい人たち

3．教師時代 ……… 28
教員免許をめざす／ビディファドの教員時代／
ダルハウジー大学──勉学と投稿の日々／
ベルモントでの教師時代──エド・シンプソンとの出会い／
ロウア・ベデックの学校での教師時代──ハーマン・リアードとの激しい恋／
理性と感情の相克／帰郷──恋愛の後日談／
キャリアウーマン／祖母の面倒を見る日々

4．『赤毛のアン』の成功──作家への道 ……… 47
『赤毛のアン』の創作／『赤毛のアン』──ストーリー紹介／『赤毛のアン』の出版／
ユーアン・マクドナルドとの結婚／結婚式から新婚旅行へ／
牧師の妻として、作家として

5．アン、その後 ……… 62
『アンの愛情』／『アンの夢の家』／『虹の谷のアン』／
『アンの娘リラ』／新しい主人公──エミリー／書き続ける理由／
ノーヴァル／バラと『青い城』／マリーゴールドとパット／
旅路の果て／まとめ

II 作品小論 ……… 75
『赤毛のアン』とカナダ的要素／『赤毛のアン』の憂鬱／
『赤毛のアン』の普遍性／『赤毛のアン』と日本／
『赤毛のアン』──多文化社会のアイデンティティ

III 作品鑑賞 ……… 85
年表・参考文献 ……… 127
索引 ……… 132
あとがき ……… 134

I

その生涯
── 人と作品 ──

L.M. Montgomery

はじめに

モンゴメリの日記

　ルーシー・モード・モンゴメリ（Lucy Maud Montgomery, 1874-1942）は、彼女自身の子ども時代の体験や夢をたくさん織り込んで『赤毛のアン』（*Anne of Green Gables*, 1908）を創作した。その強烈に個性的で、存在感のある主人公は、後にマーク・トウェイン（Mark Twain, 1835-1910）から「不滅のアリス以降フィクションに登場したもっとも愛すべき子ども」(the dearest, and the most lovable child in fiction since the immortal Alice; Eggleston, *The Greem Gables Letters*, p.80) と激賞された。アンのイメージがあまりにも鮮明なためか、『アン』の読者は、作者にアンのイメージを重ね合わせて、モンゴメリのことはすっかり知っていると錯覚しがちである。

　モンゴメリには、元来内面をさらけ出さない性向があった。特に『赤毛のアン』の成功以降は、「『アン』の作者」として振るまったので、その仮面の下を周囲のものが覗くのは難しかったはずである。あるとき、モンゴメリの特別記事を担当したトロントの新聞記者が、彼女に履歴書、幼年時代、執筆を始めた時期と理由などを尋ねる手紙を送った。それに対してモンゴメリは日記に次のように記している。

　　じゃあ、記者が知りたがっている事実だけは教えよう。でも、本当の私や私の人生についてそれ以上、その記者も新聞の読者も知ることはないだろう。それを知るカギは、この日記の中だけにあるの。

　　Well, I'll give him the bare facts he wants. He will not know any more about the real *me* or my real life for it all, nor will his readers. The only key to *that* is found in this old journal.（『モンゴメリ日記』1908年11月10日、以下SJ 1908.11.10）

　実際、日記が公開されるまで、モンゴメリに関する資料も少なかった。彼女自身の手になる『険しい道』(*The Alpine Path*, 1974) を含む、数冊の伝記、そしてペンフレンドとの間で交わされた書簡集がある程度であった。しかし、モンゴメリは読者の前にその真の姿を現しつつある。というのは、彼女が生前50余年にわたり書き綴り、遺言によって死後50年間は公開を禁止されていた膨大な日記がメアリー・ルビオ（Mary Rubio）らにより『モンゴメリ日記』(*The Selected Journals of L.M. Montgomery*) として編集され、1985年よりオックフォード大学出版局から出版されつつあるからである。この日記により『赤毛のアン』出版の経緯など、モンゴメリの生涯に関してこれまで不明であった点が容易に解明されるのである。

　たとえば、1890年、再婚した父親を訪ね、モンゴメリは西部のプリンス・アルバートへ旅をする。これについて、伝記作者の一人M. ギレン（Mollie Gillen）は『運命の紡ぎ車』(*The Wheel of Things*, 1983) の中で、当時の交通関係の資料を詳細に調べ上げ、3つのルートを洗い出し、モンゴメリはその一つを選択したであろうと推測している。一方、モンゴメリの日記を見れば、この旅の全行程は一目瞭然であり、彼女が開通まもないカナダ太平洋鉄道を利用していることがわかる。一事が万事であり、モンゴメリ関係の資料を利用する際には、日記刊行以前に出版されているもの、また刊行後も日記を参照していないものに関しては注意が必要である。

　『日記』の刊行により、カナダの内外を問わず、モンゴメリは、にわかに脚光を浴び、目を見張る勢いでモンゴメリ研究が

進展している。彼女の故郷にあるプリンス・エドワード島大学は、1994年以降、「L.M. モンゴメリ国際学会」（Biennial International Conference of L.M. Montgomery）を隔年に開催している。このようなモンゴメリ研究の成果が多数出版されているので、そのうち重要なものは本書巻末の「参考文献」に紹介する。

モンゴメリは14歳になった1889年から1942年に亡くなるまで、「何か書く価値がある」（作品鑑賞日記1参照）折りに日記をつけていた。それは日々の身の回りの出来事の単なる記録ではなく、公私にわたって彼女がどのように感じたかという記録でもある。中にはそのままエッセーあるいは短編小説と呼ぶに相応しい記載も少なくない。これより以前、「ほんの9歳」（作品鑑賞日記1参照）のころよりモンゴメリはすでに日記を書き始めている。これは、たまたま読んだウォルター・T・グレイ（Walter T. Gray）の『悪い子の日記』（*A Bad Boy's Diary*, 1880）に触発されたためである。残念なことに、この初期の日記は本人により焼却処分されてしまった。そのため現存するのは、1889年からの日記である。しかし、これには最初の日記への言及や14歳以前の回想もしばしば織り込まれている。モンゴメリの抜群の記憶力は生後20か月のときの出来事である母親との死別、言葉を喋り出す前の0歳児のころのことまで覚えているので、日記から彼女のほぼ全生涯を知ることができる。

モンゴメリは1904年1月3日の日記に、「寂しい人だけが日記を書く」（It is the *lonely* people who keep diaries.）と記している。日記は孤独な少女にとって、全幅の信頼のおける腹心の友であり、ときには不満のはけ口であった。彼女は書くことにより、一種のカタルシスを得るタイプであり、たとえ辛く、苦しい時代でも日記を書き続けた。「書くと気が楽になる。い

つもそうだ」（I think it will help me to "write it out". It always does. SJ 1898.4.8）からである。日記はついにはモンゴメリの生涯を通じての精神の安全弁となったのである。

　モンゴメリの日記はリーガルサイズの元帳10冊に約200万語をもって記録されている。その膨大な量と職業作家の手になる記録であるため、単に『赤毛のアン』の作者の生涯がわかるばかりでなく、百年前の建国期カナダの社会や当時のカナダ女性の生き方や考え方を知る資料としても興味深く、価値が高いものである。

　克明に記録された日記は、モンゴメリが後年作品を創造する際に有力な資料となった。彼女は日記を利用して自己の子ども時代へ舞い戻り、子ども独特の思考方法や感情に触れることができたのである。本書では日記が実際の作品に利用されている例を「作品鑑賞」に挙げているので参照されたい。

　『日記』のオリジナルは、現在カナダのグウェルフ大学（University of Guelph）のL.M. モンゴメリ・コレクション（L.M. Montgomery Collection）に所蔵され、1992年より一般公開されている。2004年に『日記』の最終巻（第5巻）が刊行され、ついにモンゴメリの全生涯が明らかになった。

モンゴメリの故郷──プリンス・エドワード島

　モンゴメリがこよなく愛し、アンが「世界で一番美しいところ」と賞賛したプリンス・エドワード島（Prince Edward Island）は、カナダ東部、セント・ローレンス湾の南に位置している。その昔、先住民からセント・ローレンス湾の波間に浮かぶゆりかごと呼ばれたこの島は、面積わずか5660平方キロ、人口約13万人（1990年）の小さな島であるが、れっきとしたカナダ連邦の一州である。

この島はもともと、サン・ジャン島と呼ばれていたが、1798年プリンス・エドワード島と改名される。イギリス国王ジョージ3世の王子（プリンス）で、のちにヴィクトリア女王の父親となるエドワードにちなんだものである。
　カナダの近代史はこの小さな島から始まったと言っても過言ではない。1864年カナダ各植民地から、後にカナダ連邦結成の父祖と呼ばれた傑出した政治家たちがプリンス・エドワード島のシャーロットタウン（Charlottetown）に参集し、自治領としてイギリスからの独立を討議する建国会議が開かれたからである。このシャーロットタウン会議を皮切りに幾つかの会議等を経て、1867年カナダ連邦が結成された。プリンス・エドワード島はカナダ連邦発祥の地となったのである。もっとも、プリンス・エドワード島が連邦に加盟したのは、9年あとの1873年のことである。その翌年、モンゴメリは誕生している。父方の祖父ドナルド・モンゴメリ（Donald Montgomery）は1874年から1893年までオタワの国会でプリンス・エドワード島選出の上院議員を務めた。
　酸化鉄を含む赤土と木々の緑が印象的なプリンス・エドワード島の自然は今も昔も変わっていない。

　　今や世界はとっても素敵。まさに素晴らしい春が始まらんとするところ。リンゴ園は桃色がかって赤らみ、桜の木は香りよい雪の花冠のよう。朝、新鮮な湿った風は、リンゴや桜のいい香りとモミの樹皮のかすかな香りで目まいがするほど快い。野原は緑のビロードを敷きつめたようで、カバやカエデの木は緑の葉の重いカーテンを揺すっている。ああ、なんと美しい世界！

　　Oh, the world is so lovely now. It is the very prime

of glorious springtide. The apple orchards are a pinky blush, the cherry trees are wreaths of perfumed snow; and in the mornings the fresh moist air is dizzily sweet with their delicious odors and resinous breaths of fir. The fields are like breadths of green velvet and birches and maples swing heavy curtains of green leaves. Oh, it's a dear beautiful world!（SJ 1893.6.9）

　海は青から灰色に変り、さざ波が足元でぱちゃぱちゃと音を立てていた。夕焼けは光りかがやいてはいなかったが、その壮麗さは荒々しく、陰鬱で、人を魅了するところがあった。太陽は赤らんだ金色の光を後に残しながら地平線近くの黒雲の峰に沈んだ。一方雲の下には火のように真っ赤な筋が流れていて、ところどころに金色と緋色の小さな雲が点在していた。

　The sea changed from blue to gray and the little waves plashed at our feet. The sunset was not brilliant but there was a sort of savage, sullen fascinating grandeur about it. The sun sank in a low bank of black cloud, leaving a wake of rosy gold, while below the cloud ran a strip of fiery crimson, flecked here and there with tiny cloudlets of gold and scarlet.（SJ 1890.6.7）

モンゴメリの心に深く刻まれたプリンス・エドワード島の風景は、名作『赤毛のアン』を生む要因となった。彼女は『アン』の執筆にあたり、島の自然とみずからの子ども時代の経験を織り混ぜて作品を創作することにした。その目論見はみごとに成功し、プリンス・エドワード島は、世界の文学地図に永久

に記されることになったのである。

　毎年、日本をはじめ世界各国から大勢の観光客がこの名作の舞台を一目見ようとプリンス・エドワード島を訪れている。これまでは空路とフェリーでしかこの島へのアクセスはなかったが、1997年6月から「コンフェデレーション橋」を利用して、本土から陸路で島に渡ることが可能となった。州都シャーロットタウンにある芸術センター（Confederation Centre of the Arts）内の劇場では、夏期の間「赤毛のアン」のミュージカルが上演され、好評を得ている。シャーロットタウンから車で40分ほど北西に行ったところに、モンゴメリが育ったキャヴェンディシュ（Cavendish）がある。ここでは彼女が住んだ家の跡や『赤毛のアン』のモデルとなった家を見学することができる。作品に登場する「恋人の小径」（Lover's Lane）や「おばけの森」（Haunted Wood）の散策もできる。キャヴェンディシュの近隣のニューロンドンには、「モンゴメリの生家」があり、パークコーナーには、モンゴメリが結婚式を挙げ、現在は博物館になっている「銀の森屋敷」（Silver Bush）がある。島にはほかにも『赤毛のアン』関連のスポットが多数あり、プリンス・エドワード島は「アン」を愛する人々の憧れの聖地となっている。

1．子ども時代

誕生

　1769年、ヒュー・モンゴメリと名乗る男性が妻のメアリー・マクシャノンとともにスコットランドからプリンス・エドワード島に移住してきた。彼はプリンスタウン（現在のモールペック）で英語を母語とする最初の移民であったといわれる。一方、1782年シャーロットタウンに赤ん坊が生まれ、ウィリアム・シンプソン・マクニールと名付けられた。彼は後にこの地で生まれた最初の男児であると自称した。

　プリンス・エドワード島への最初期の入植者であるこの両名家を先祖に持つヒュー・ジョン・モンゴメリ（Hugh John Montgomery）とクレアラ・ウルナー・マクニール（Clara Woolner Macneill）の間に、一人の女の子が1874年11月30日、クリフトン（現在のニューロンドン）で産声をあげた。この子こそ、後に名作『赤毛のアン』を世に送ることになるL.M. モンゴメリであった。一家が過ごし、モンゴメリが後年、以下のように懐かしんだ家は、現在も残っている。

　　そしてある角を曲がると、道端に小さな黄色がかった茶色の家がある。私はいつもその家をちょっとうっとりとしてながめる。というのも、それは私の両親が新婚生活をはじめた家であり、私が生まれ、私の人生の最初の年を過ごした家だから。

　　And here, around a certain corner, is a certain small, yellowish-brown house, close to the road, that I always look at with a kind of fascination, for it is the house where my father and mother lived after their marriage, and where I was born and spent the first year of my life.（SJ 1898.12.31）

母との死別

　残念ながらモンゴメリはこの家に長く住むことはなかった。というのも、彼女が生後20か月のときに、母親が結核で亡くなったからである。残された幼子は大変聡明で、抜群の記憶力の持ち主であった。なにしろ言葉を覚える以前の記憶、たとえば、おしおきに部屋に閉じ込められたとき、椅子に睨まれて恐いと感じたこと、町の写真屋で椅子にかけられた毛皮の肘掛けが恐くて泣きじゃくったことなどをしっかり覚えているのであるから。

　人並はずれた記憶力を持つために、ときには普通の子どもより早く人生の苦しみを味わわなければならないこともあった。2歳足らずのモンゴメリは、母親との死別のシーンをしっかり記憶している。彼女はこのとき自分が白いモスリンのドレスを着ていたこと、部屋の中の様子やそこに漂う独特の雰囲気、棺の中に横たわる母の死顔などを鮮明に覚えているのである。それと母親に触れたときの奇妙な冷たさも。可哀想にモンゴメリが母親に直に触れた記憶は、後にも先にも、このときだけしかないのである。（作品鑑賞日記2参照）

祖父母との生活

　その後、父親がプリンス・アルバートへ移り住み、そこで再婚したために、モンゴメリはキャヴェンディシュに住み、農場主兼郵便局長であった母方の祖父アレグザーンダー・マクニールとその妻ルーシー・ウルナーにひきとられることになった。すでに6人の子どもを育て上げ、50歳をゆうに過ぎた老夫妻は、期せずして格別の知能と豊かな感受性を兼ね備えた孫娘を育て

る羽目に陥ったのである。祖父母は熱心な長老派教会信徒であった。当時、スコットランド長老派は、真面目で、事務的であり、人生をおもしろおかしく生きるような人々ではなかった。特に作り話などは認めなかった。したがって、老祖父母はつねに長老派教会信徒としての内省的な生活を孫娘にも要求し、厳しくしつけた。

プリンス・エドワード島はスコットランドからの移民の多い島であるが、とりわけモンゴメリの祖先はすでに述べたように、父方も母方も1700年代に彼の地から移住してきた由緒正しい家系であり、その一族は島の発展と深くかかわってきた。祖父母はモンゴメリに名家の子女に相応しい気位と自尊心を持つように養育した。彼女自身、上流階級に属すること、ひいてはみずからの家系が「ノルマン人のイングランド征服」(Norman Conquest) にまで遡る古いものであることに強い誇りを感じていた。モンゴメリは養祖父母の期待にこたえるように、慎み深く、どんなときにも本心を曝け出さない若者に成長した。

しかし、後年、「子どもが老人に養育されるのはひじょうに不幸だ」(It is a great misfortune for a child to be brought up by old people. SJ 1905.1.2) と成長期の若者が老人との暮らしの中で体験した苦労を述懐している。

ただし、マクニール夫妻は孫娘に物質的には何不自由をさせなかった。1881年に入学したキャヴェンディシュ小学校のクラスでブーツをはいていたのは、モンゴメリだけであり、それはほかの生徒の羨望の的であった。もっとも、モンゴメリ自身は、みんなと同じように素足で学校へ行くことを望んでいたのだが。また当時、キャヴェンディシュで果樹園があるのは、マクニール家くらいだったので、リンゴを持ってクラスへでかければ、交換に大抵のものを手に入れることができた。

孤独な少女時代——空想の世界への逃避

　物質的には満たされていても、幼くして両親の保護を離れた少女は孤独であった。それを癒すために、空想の世界に逃避することがしばしばであった。『赤毛のアン』の中で、本箱のガラス扉に映る自分の顔をガラスの奥に住む友達ケイティ・モーリスにみたてて、アンが話しかける場面がある。それは、居間に置いてある本箱の左の扉にケイティ・モーリス、右の扉にルーシー・グレーという未亡人の友達を持っていた幼き日のモンゴメリの姿そのものである（作品鑑賞日記 5 参照）。

◇モンゴメリ 11 歳のころ。

読書の喜び

　　それに私は、その当時も今も、2つの素晴らしい逃避と
　　慰めをもっている——自然と本の世界。

　　I had besides, then as now, two great refuges and consolations——the world of nature and the world of books.（SJ 1905.1.2）

　幼くして両親と離別する悲運に見舞われた少女に、読書は逃避と慰めを与えた。そんなモンゴメリはいつしか、自分で本が買えるようになるから早く大人になりたい、たくさん本を買える大人になりたいと将来を夢見るようになる。10代のとき、友達から借りたモルト・フーケ男爵の美しい水の精と騎士の恋物語『オンディーヌ』（*Undine*, 1811）を授業中にこっそりと

読んで、モンゴメリは密かに誓いをたてたものであった。大人になったら、絶対に、この本を買おうと。その後、シャーロットタウンのカーター書店で『オンディーヌ』を見つけ、勝ち誇った気分で家に買って帰ったのは、26歳のときであった。そして子ども時代に楽しんだ『アンデルセン童話集』(*Anndersen's Fairy Tales*)をとうとう英国に注文し、手に入れたのは、35歳も過ぎたときのことである。

　当時、プリンス・エドワード島で本を入手することは、それほど容易ではなかった。それでも知的な人々は文芸協会を組織して、図書を共同購入し、会員間で回覧していた。というわけで、モンゴメリの読書も同じ作品を繰り返し読むことが多かった。幸い彼女はそれを嫌ってはいなかった。「私は本が大好き！一度だけでなく、何度も何度も繰り返して読む。10回繰り返して読んでも、はじめて読んだ時のように楽しい。本は素晴らしい世界だ」(How I do love books! Not merely to read once but over and over again. I enjoy the tenth reading of a book as much as the first. Books are a delightful world in themselves. SJ 1893.1.12) と日記に記している。そればかりか、モンゴメリは年月を経て同じ作品を再読したときに、その作品に対する自分の評価がどのように変化しているか発見するのを読書の楽しみの一つとしていた。中年になって『アンデルセン童話集』を再読した彼女は、作品の変わらぬ魅力とともに、それをいまだ楽しめる自分を発見して感激している。

　さらに、モンゴメリにとって読書後の醍醐味は、作品から金言警句や気に入った箇所を抜き取り、専用のノートに書き写すことであった。『赤毛のアン』には、注意深く読むと、ブラウニング (Robert Browning)、バイロン (George Gordon Byron)、テニソン (Alfred Tennyson)、ワーズワース (William Wordsworth)、シェイクスピア (William Shakespeare)、ホイッティア（John Greenleaf Whittier）、スコット（Walter Scott）等の作品や聖書からの引用が満天の星のごとく散りばめられている。

　一冊の作品を大事に、丁寧に読み、そのエッセンスを的確に読み手の血肉にしていくという読書法の結果であろう。モンゴメリは次第に、ある作品が古典になるかどうかは、子どもから大人まで楽しませることができるかどうかだという確信を得ていくのである。

書く喜び

　　オタワでテリトリーズのシュルツ副総督に会ったモンゴメリおじいちゃんの話では、副総督はサスカチェワンについての私の記事を読み、大変誉めて、おじいちゃんに私の写真やその後書いたものがあったらくれるよう頼んで欲しいと言ったという。光栄の至りではありませんか。

　　Grandpa Montgomery was telling me that he had met Lieutenant Governor Schultz of the Territories in Ottawa and that he had read my article on Saskatchewan and admired it very much; and he told grandpa to ask me for my photo and anything I might have written since. Quite a compliment for little me, isn't it?（SJ 1892.7.17）

　このモンゴメリ17歳のときの日記が示すように、彼女は子どものころよりたぐい希な文才の持ち主であった。10代のモンゴメリは学校から『モントリオール・ウィットネス』（*The Montreal Witness*）誌主催の作文コンクールにしばしば応募し、「レフォルス岬の伝説」（"The Legend of Cape Leforce"）

や「マルコポーロ号の遭難」("The Wreck of the Marco Polo") と題する作品は優秀な成績をおさめた。

モンゴメリの文才は母方から受け継いだものであろう。マクニール家には詩人やストーリーテリングの才能に長けた人たちが多かった。とくに大叔母のメアリー・ローソンは生来のストーリーテラーであり、モンゴメリのストーリーテリングの才能に少なからず影響を及ぼした人物である。

モンゴメリ自身が後にしばしば述べているが、彼女には相反する二つの血――つまり、情熱的で想像力豊かなモンゴメリ家の血筋と清教徒マクニール家の良心――が流れている。どちらも片方を圧倒するほど強くはなかった。日常生活において、モンゴメリはマクニールの家風に従い、慎み深く暮らさなければならなかった。すると、モンゴメリ家の血が、そのはけ口を求めて騒ぎ出すのだった。この相反する血の葛藤に、モンゴメリはその後の人生において幾度となく苦悩することになるが、幼いモンゴメリは、そのディレンマの解消を「書くこと」に見い出したのであった。

そしていつしか、詩や小説を書いては新聞社や雑誌社へ送る、ある種の「投稿魔」となった。自分の作品が活字になることは、彼女にとって大きな喜びであった。成功よりは不成功の方が多かったが、幸い祖父が自宅で郵便局を経営していたので、だれにも気づかれないうちに雑誌に投稿することができたのであった。

作家になる決心

投稿を繰り返すうちに、文学少女は原稿が収入源となり、将来、文筆で身を立てられるかもしれないと思うようになる。のちには、ニューヨークの『レディーズ・ワールド』(*Ladies' World*) 誌に「スミレだけが」("Only a Violet") という詩を

送ったところ採用され、2人分の予約購読料を得ている。たとえわずかでも、謝礼や原稿料は彼女にとり、とても励みになった。

　モンゴメリのように聡明な子どもは、ほとんど孤児のような境遇の中で、早くから将来の自立を考えていたに違いない。女性の社会進出がまだ活発でなかった当時、女性がつける職業は限られていた。また、モンゴメリの場合は、名門の出身というプライドもあり、なりふりかまわずに働くわけにはいかなかった。そんな彼女にとって作家という職業は、ひじょうに魅力的に映ったに違いない。

　実は、日記はモンゴメリが将来作家になることを10代初めから意識し始めていたことを明らかにしている。ひそかに詩や物語をたくさん書き溜めていた少女は、そのうち自分の作品に対する他人の批評を聞きたいと思うようになった。そこでモンゴメリは12歳のとき、「夕べの夢」（"Evening Dreams"）という自作の詩を当時マクニール家に下宿していたロビンソン先生に、さりげなく差し出してみた。

　「先生、こんな歌、ごぞんじですか？」

　　静かに西の彼方に
　　夕日が沈みゆくころ
　　虹をなす栄光の輪のなかに
　　座してわが身を休ませる

　　現在と未来を忘れ
　　いまいちど過ぎし日に生きん
　　我が両眼にうるわしき古い日々を映して　　（山口昌子訳）

　"When the evening sun is setting

Quietly in the west
In a halo of rainbow glory,
I sit me down to rest.

I forget the present and future,
I live over the past once more
As I see before me crowding
The beautiful days of yore." (SJ 1901.3.21)

　すると、ちょっとした歌い手でもあった先生は、「その歌は聞いたことはないけれど、とても美しい歌詞ね」と答えたという。
　モンゴメリは先生のさりげない一言に大いに勇気づけられた。そこで、将来は作家になろうと決心し、文学の小道に一歩を踏み出したのであった。後年の人気作家誕生の裏には、大人の子どもに対するちょっとした励ましの言葉があったのである。

2．10代のビッグ・イベント

西部への旅

　1890年夏、15歳のモンゴメリはサスカチェワンのプリンス・アルバート（Prince Albert）で再婚している父親と暮らすため、まだ見たことのない継母や義理の妹に不安と期待を抱きながら、西部へ向かう。

　　明日出発するので興奮している——そして、ちょっと憂鬱でもある。これまで旅行をしたことはないが、きっと好きになると思う。でもプリンス・アルバートはどうかしら？気に入るかな？それに義理のお母さんはどうかしら？わからない。手紙からすると、良さそうな人だけど。できることなら、彼女を愛そう。本当の母のように。

　　I feel excited about starting away to-morrow——and a little blue, too. I've never travelled any but I think I'll like *that*; but what about Prince Albert? Shall I like it? And my stepmother? I do not know. She seems nice from her letters and I mean to love her if I can, just as if she were really my mother.（SJ 1890.8.8）

　15歳の少女は、開通間もないカナダ太平洋鉄道に乗って、遠く離れた西部の町へ一人旅をしたのであった。旅の途中では、プリンス・エドワード島選出の上院議員である祖父と親交のあったカナダの初代首相ジョン・A. マクドナルド卿（Sir John A. Macdonald）とも出会っている。

　　ケンジントンに着くと、ジョン・マクドナルド卿夫妻

──島を巡歴中──を乗せた特別列車が一時間以内に到着するという。そこで、おじいちゃん──上院議員であり、卿の親友──は、ケンジントンで私たちを同乗させて欲しいという電報をハンター・リバーへ打った。カナダの首相にお目にかかれるかと思うと、どんなに興奮したことか。お二人を乗せた特別列車が到着すると、私はおじいちゃんに続いて乗車した。そして、次の瞬間には首相ご本人の目の前にいたのだった。首相は大変やさしい方で、夫人とご自分の間に坐るよう促された。私はかしこまってそこに坐り横目でじろじろとお二人をながめた。

Finally we reached Kensington where we were informed that a special containing Sir John and Lady Macdonald——who are touring the Island——would be along in an hour; so Grandpa——who is a Senator and a great crony of Sir John's——telegraphed to Hunter River for Sir John to stop at Kensington and take us on. I assure you I was quite excited over the prospect of seeing the Premier of Canada. When the special came I followed grandpa on board and the next moment was in the presence of the great man himself. He was very genial and motioned me to a seat between himself and Lady M. where I sat demurely and scrutinized them both out of the tail of my eye. (SJ 1890.8.11)

モンゴメリが見た今から百年以上前のモントリオール、トロント、ウィニペッグなどのカナダの町の記述には、興味深いものがある。たとえば、以下の記述は、モンゴメリがカナダ太平洋鉄道に乗ってモントリオール入りし、一流ホテルに到着した

ところである。彼女の故郷に電気がまだ引かれていなかった1890年に、モントリオールはすでに電気で明るく照らされた都会であったことがわかる。

　大きなセントローレンス・ホールにいる。セントローレンス川にかかるC.P.R.の吊り橋を渡りながら見た景色は壮大だった。ここに5時半頃に到着した。人でごった返している通りは電気であかあかと照らされていた。ここでは英語と同じくらいフランス語を耳にする。

　Here we are in the big St. Lawrence Hall. The views you see when crossing the St. Lawrence River on the C.P.R. suspension bridge are magnificent. We got there about 5.30. The thronged streets were brilliantly lighted by electricity. You hear as much French as English here. (SJ 1890.8.13)

　自伝『険しい道』の中でモンゴメリは、プリンス・アルバートに関しては、1年間滞在し、高等学校へ通ったとしか言及していない。しかし、実際は、ここでの生活は辛いものであった。彼女と余り年の違わない年若い継母は、モンゴメリにはむっつりしていて、嫉妬深く、分別のない人で、絶えずあら探しをし、不平を言い、難癖を付けて父の人生を惨めにしていると映った。

　継母の方も、突然、大きな娘の

◇モンゴメリ17歳のころ。

親となったことで、自分が老けて見えるのを嫌い、モンゴメリが髪の毛をアップにすることを禁じた。また子守を押しつけ、家事手伝いをさせ、学校へもろくに通わせなかった。さらに外出するときには、つまみ食いをされないように食料貯蔵室に鍵をかける念の入れようだった。

西部で出会った忘れがたい人たち

　プリンス・アルバート滞在中にも、モンゴメリには忘れがたい人たちとの出会いがあった。彼女はウィルとその姉のローラという親友を得た。ウィルは赤毛で緑の目、ゆがんだ口をしていて、どう見てもハンサムではないが、素敵で、とてもおもしろい青年であった。モンゴメリはウィルのことを恋愛感情なしで好いていた。

　　　これまで会った男性のうちでウィルがいちばん**好き**だけど、愛していないことはわかっている。彼はちょうど兄弟か、愉快な仲間のようだ。

　　　I *like* Will better than any boy I ever met but I *know* I don't love him——he just seems like a brother or a jolly good comrade to me.（SJ 1891.7.5）

　モンゴメリは学生時代に、おそらく愛読書であった『パンジー』（*Pansy*）シリーズ（本書119頁注14参照）の影響であろう、多くの友人と「10年間開封禁止書簡」とでも呼ぶべき手紙を交わして楽しんでいた。当時のモンゴメリに、この種の手紙は素敵で、ロマンチックに映っていたようだ。

　しかし、その後10年を待たずして、ウィルと交換した書簡は開封されることになる。1897年ウィルの訃報を聞き、モン

ゴメリは彼との再会を切なく望むのであった。

　　封筒をあけたときの気持ちは表現しようがない。手紙は死者からの——霊界からの——メッセージのように思えた。それはラブレターだった。それまでの普通の手紙ではみせようともしなかった、とても素敵な調子で語っていた。ああ、それを読んで、かわいそうな一人ぼっちの私が、どんなに傷ついたことだろう！

　　I cannot describe my feelings as I opened the envelope. The letter seemed like a message from the dead ——from the world of spirits. It was a letter of love, speaking more plainly than he had ever ventured to do in ordinary letters, and oh, how it hurt poor lonely me to read it!（SJ 1897.4.15）

容姿端麗で頭脳明晰、しかも慎み深く、いかなる場合でも本心を全面的にさらけ出すことのなかったモンゴメリは、多くの異性から好意を寄せられた。プリンス・アルバートでは担任のマスタード先生（Mr. Mustard）を夢中にさせ、先生のプライドを傷つけずにその求婚を思い止まらせるのに苦労したものだった。

　　今夜、マスタード先生はいそいそとやって来て9時から11時までいた。猫に引っかかせてやりたかった。先生は内心を打ち明けるように、東部へ行ってカレッジに入るといった。それから先どんな職業に付いたらいいと思うかと私にたずねた！くすくす笑いたかったが、なんとかこらえ、何食わぬ顔をして、とてもまじめに答えた。（中略）

するとM先生は、ノックス・カレッジに行って、牧師になるつもりだとおどおどと言った。私は先生の前でどうやって笑いをこらえたものか分からなかった。マスタードが牧師ですって‼
　ああ――なんたる響き――マスタード牧師様！その名前の組み合わせの前に「ミセス」と書く運命にある気の毒な女性に同情するわ。

　This evening Mr. Mustard came shuffling along at nine and stayed till eleven. I wished the cats had him. He was quite confidential and said he was going down east to go to college. He then asked me what profession I thought he'd better follow! I felt like snickering but managed to keep a straight face and said very gravely, ...
　And then Mr. M. sheepishly informed me that he was thinking of going to Knox College and meant to be a minister. I don't know how I kept from laughing right out in his face. Mustard a minister‼ Oh Lordy――how it will sound――Rev. Mr. Mustard. I pity the poor woman whose fate it will be to write "Mrs." before such a combination.（SJ 1891.6.6）

　マスタード先生とモンゴメリの一連のエピソードは、『赤毛のアン』（15章）の中のプリシー・アンドリューズとフィリップス先生の関係を連想させる。そして、このときのモンゴメリは、31年後に成功した先生と再会するとは、想像だにしなかったのである。
　結局、西部での生活はうまくいかず、モンゴメリは最愛の父

との生活をあきらめ、1年後の1891年9月5日に再び、プリンス・エドワード島に戻ったのであった。

　今日は全く混乱した——悲しみと喜びが半々。お父さんが今朝二階から降りて来て私にキスし、震え声で言った。「昨夜おじいちゃんから手紙がきたんだよ。おまえは再来週の月曜日か火曜日に出発することになるだろう」
　お父さんと別れると思うとせつなくて、二階へ駆け上がって泣いた。でもあの懐かしいキャヴェンディシュへ帰る**こと——これは喜ばなければならなかった**。それから、モンゴメリ夫人の、ささいだが止むことのない虐待や陰険な迫害からのがれること——どんなにほっとするだろう！

　I have felt quite mixed up to-day——sad and glad in about equal proportions. When father came downstairs this morning he kissed me and said, with a tremble in his voice,
　"I had a letter from father last night and I expect you'll have to start on Monday or Thursday week."
　I felt dreadfully over the thought of leaving father and just ran upstairs and cried. But then, to go back to dear old Cavendish——I just *had* to feel glad over that. And to escape from Mrs. Montgomery's ceaseless petty tyranny and underhand persecution——what a relief that will be! (SJ 1891.8.16)

3. 教師時代

教員免許をめざす

　作家になるべくして生まれてきたようなモンゴメリであるが、けっしてみずからの才能に溺れることはなかった。大切な才能を磨き、作家として成功する努力を惜しまなかった。将来はペンで身を立てたいと志したものの、それはけっして平坦な道のりではなかった。彼女は常に少しでも高い教育を受けて、文才を磨きたいという希望を持っていた。西部から戻った後、モンゴメリは祖父母を説得して、キャヴェンディシュのハイスクールに戻り、プリンス・オブ・ウエールズ・カレッジ（Prince of Wales College）進学と教員免許取得をめざして勉強する。

　今日はこれまでになく幸せで満足に感じている。ここの学校に再び通い、プリンス・オブ・ウェールズ・カレッジと教員免許を目指して勉強することが今日決まった。とてもうれしい。いつもこうなってほしいと願いつづけてきた。自分でなにかやらなければならないと自覚しているし、それしか道はないように思えるが、おじいちゃんとおばあちゃんがいつもひどく反対したので、だんだんやる気がなくなっていた。しかし、おじいちゃんたちがついに折れたので、新学期がはじまる来週月曜日から学校へ行く。先生はウエストさんとかいう方。もう少し教育をうけなければならないので一生懸命勉強するつもり。

　I feel happier and more contented to-day than I have felt for a long time. It was decided to-day that I am to go to school here again and study for Prince of Wales and a teacher's license. I am delighted. I have always longed for this. I realize that I must do something for myself and this seems the only thing possible but grandpa and grandma have always been so bitterly against it that I was getting discouraged. They have given in at last however and I am to begin school when it opens next Monday. A Miss West is the teacher. I mean to study very hard for I *must* get some more education. (SJ 1892.8.9)

　1893年7月18日、モンゴメリは受験者264名のうち5番という好成績でプリンス・オブ・ウエールズ・カレッジの試験に合格、その年の9月に同カレッジに入学した。
　モンゴメリは1年間で教員免許を取得、シャーロットタウンの下宿生活や学校生活は彼女の日記に生き生きと記されている。ここでも彼女は異性にもてた。一方、みずからも述べているように、たいへんプライドが高く、つねに自分の理想に照らして他人を判断する傾向のあったモンゴメリは、男友達に対する辛辣な批評を日記の中にしばしば記している。

　　カレッジに行ったおかげでジャックは大分賢くなった。ジャックはとてもいい子。だけど大して中味がない。

　College has smartened Jack up a good bit and he is very nice, although there is not a great deal in him. (SJ 1892.6.22)

　　レムはある種の職業には適してはいるが、知力や教養や躾が備わっていない。(中略) 私は今までレムとはずっと率直に親しくつき合ってきたが、それ以上のものという素

振りを見せたことは絶対ない。

　He has an aptitude of a certain sort of business but he has no brains, culture, or breeding. . . . I've always been frank and friendly with him but I've certainly never pretended to be anything else.（SJ 1894.10.22）

　1894年6月、カレッジを卒業したモンゴメリは、キャヴェンディシュに戻り就職活動を行う。しかし、当時も教職はなかなかの狭き門であり、就職活動は難航した。モンゴメリが10代になったころ、育ての親である祖父母はすでに70歳近くであったが彼らは年とともにますます頑固になり、モンゴメリの就職活動に関しても非協力的であった。

　かわいそうな私以外は、皆学校に就職したようだ。私が一生懸命努力したことは誰も知らない。20校に履歴書を送って出願したが、これまでのところ、がっくりすることに、何の反響もない。みずから出向いて学校の理事に出願することができないので、就職の機会はあまりない。他の女子学生の父親や友人は、学校へ馬車で出願に連れていってくれるが、おじいちゃんはそんなことをしてくれないだろう。また、私が自分で行くのに馬も貸してくれないだろう。だから郵便より他に手だてがない。手紙を出してもたいていは返事さえ来ない。

　Everyone but poor me can get a school, it seems. Dear knows, I've tried hard enough. I have sent applications for a score of schools, but so far the result has been discouraging silence. I cannot get to apply to the trustees in person and so I have a poor chance. Other girls' fathers drive them about to apply for schools but grandfather will not do this for me, or let me have a horse to go myself, so there is nothing for it but letters, which are generally not even answered.（SJ 1894.7.14）

ビディファドの教員時代

　1894年7月26日、モンゴメリは、ついに、教員採用通知を受け取った。勤務先は、島の西方にあるビディファド（Bideford）の小学校であった。

　学校はうまくいっている。現在38名が登録しており、その生徒たちをだんだん好きになってきている。彼らは可愛い一団で、とても親切。毎日花束をもってきてくれる子どももいて、私の机は本物の花壇のようだ。元気づけられる噂をちらほら耳にするので、生徒たちも私を好いていてくれると思う。

　School goes on well. I have 38 on the roll now and am getting fond of them all. They are nice little crowd and very obliging. Some of them bring me a bouquet every day, so that my desk is a veritable flower garden. I think they like me, too, from some encouraging reports I have heard.（SJ 1894.8.13）

　新米ではあるが、はつらつとして初々しい教師像が魅力的である。一方、日記は女教師の抱える悩みも語っている。
　ある日、モンゴメリは周囲から風変わりと汚さで物笑いの種

であるマケイ夫妻の養子、エイモスの家庭訪問をする。

> 老婦人は買った日から一度も洗ったことがないようなカップにお茶を注いだ。カップの内側も外側も古い茶渋が惜しみなくついていた。私はカップのきれいなところを見つけて飲もうとしたが、無駄であった。そこで、目をつむり、ぐっと飲んだ。ほぼ飲みかけたとき見たものは、何という光景、泥の海に浮かぶ氷山のように、**サワークリームの巨大な塊が浮遊しているひどいお茶だった。**（中略）そこで私は厚さがたっぷり一インチもあるパンを取った。それにはバターがこってり塗ってあった——**なんて**バター！その中に髪の毛を3本見つけた。（中略）その恐ろしい食事を**絶対**に忘れないだろう。

> The old lady poured out tea in cups which looked as if they had never been washed since the day they were bought. Inside and out they were liberally daubed with ancient tea-stains. I tried vainly to find a clean spot to drink from and, failing, shut my eyes and took a wild gulp, the taste nearly finishing what the sight had begun, for it was an atrocious brew with huge lumps of *sour* cream floating round like ice-bergs in a muddy sea. ... So I took a huge slice of bread fully an inch thick, plastered on some butter——*such* butter! I found three hairs in it : ... I shall *never* forget that awful meal. (SJ 1895.6.6)

ビディファドの小学校に就職したのもつかの間、モンゴメリはさらに高い教育をめざす。

ほんとうの大学で1年間過ごしたい。それは作家になりたいという私の志望に役立つと思うから。

　　I am anxious to spend a year at a real college as I think it would help me along in my ambition to be a writer.（SJ 1895.4.20）

　しかし、周囲の目は必ずしも女性の高等教育に好意的ではなかった。祖父は孫娘の進学にまったく無関心であったし、女性の分際で「説教師」にでもなりたいのかと揶揄する者もいた。そんなときモンゴメリは、

　　その意見を尊敬できる友達が一人でもいて——私に「あなたは正しい。もし知的な訓練を受けたら、あなたはなにかを成し遂げることができる。がんばりなさい！」と言ってくれる人がいれば、なんと励まされることだろう！

　　If I had just *one* friend, whose opinion I valued——to say to me "You are right. You have it in you to achieve something if you get the proper intellectual training. Go ahead!" what a comfort it could be!（SJ 1895.9.15）

と思うのであった。
　1895年、モンゴメリはさらなる教育の機会を求めて、ビディファドの学校を辞職する。

ダルハウジー大学——勉学と投稿の日々

　1895年9月17日、モンゴメリはノヴァスコシア州ハリファ

ックスにあるダルハウジー大学（Dalhousie University）に進学し、英文学の選択コースを1年間履修する。文学士課程を修了する経済的余裕はなかった。モンゴメリは大学の勉強と投稿を繰り返す作家志願の日々を送る。

　1896年2月15日、モンゴメリはイブニング・メイル紙の「日常的な苦労や試練において、忍耐強いのは、男か女か」という課題の作文コンテストに応募し、めでたく受賞した。その獲得賞金で、テニソン、ロングフェロー、ホイッティア、バイロンの作品を買い揃えている。いつも身近に置いておいて、あきのこないものが欲しかったからである。また、フィラデルフィアの雑誌『ゴールデン・デイズ』（*Golden Days*）に投稿した短編小説「お祭り騒ぎ」（"Our Charivari"）で5ドルの原稿料を手にしている。その後も『ユース・コンパニオン』（*The Youth's Companion*）等の雑誌に投稿し、原稿料を得ている。

　モンゴメリの作家としての成功は、単に才能と教育の賜ばかりではない。彼女の並々ならぬ努力が勝利へと導いたのだ。華氏零下20度の部屋で凍死しそうになりながらもペンを置くことなく、困難のもとでも文学を追求しなければならないと努力を重ね、成功を夢見る。

　　　文学の道は、最初はとても遅々としている。しかし、私は、昨年の今頃に比べ、非常に進歩した。そして、成功するまで、辛抱強く仕事をするつもりだ――遅かれ早かれ――世に認められ、成功すると信じているから。

　　　The road of literature is at first a very slow one, but I have made a good deal of progress since this time last year and I mean to work patiently on until I win ――as I believe I shall, sooner or later――recognition and success.（SJ 1897.4.9）

モンゴメリの己を信じ、ひたむきに作家としての成功を求める姿には、心打たれるものがある。

ベルモントでの教師時代——エド・シンプソンとの出会い

ダルハウジー大学のコースを終えると、モンゴメリは再び、ベルモントの学校で教鞭をとることになった。そこではエド・シンプソン（Edwin Simpson）という男性教員が教えていたが、彼が秋からカッレジへ行くことになったので、モンゴメリはその後任として採用されたのである。

プリンス・エドワード島の御三家といえば、最初に入植したマクニール家、クラーク家、シンプソン家であった。エドはこのシンプソン家の御曹司であった。モンゴメリはこのエドと、子どものころに彼女の親戚が大勢住むパーク・コーナーで出会っている。

エドはハンサムで賢く善良で教養があった。将来は医者か、弁護士か、牧師をめざしている青年であった。ところで、モンゴメリは日頃から男性に次のような理想像を抱いていた。

>　私が**愛せる**と思う男性の理想像——もちろん、ハンサム——どんな子でも不格好な恋人を夢見るかしら？——教養があって、生まれも社会的地位も私と同じくらい——そして、なかでも最も大切なのは——知性が同じくらいの人。とくに知性が重要！　少なくとも知力に関して、私と釣り合わなければ、相手をけっして愛せないと思った。

>　I had an ideal——a visionary dream of the man I thought I *could* love——handsome, of course——did ever girl dream of a plain lover?——educated, my equal in

birth and social position and ——most important of all ——in intellect. On that last I laid particular stress. Never, so I fancied, could I care for a man who could not meet me on equal ground at least in the matter of mental power!（SJ 1898.4.8）

　エドはモンゴメリの理想の男性像に合致していたばかりか、彼女をひじょうに愛していた。幼いころに両親の庇護から離れたモンゴメリにとり、エドは家庭の安らぎを与えてくれるかのように思われた。

　　ようするに彼といっしょに暮らせば、たいへん満足できるだろうと思った。彼は賢かった。学問的職業の一つにつくために勉強していた。したがって彼の妻になれば、よい社会的地位と、私の趣味にあった生活が保障されるだろう。

　　In short, I thought life with him would be a very satisfactory existence. Ed was clever; he was studying for one of the learned professions and consequently his wife would have a good social position and a life in accordance with my tastes.（SJ 1897.6.30）

　エドは1897年2月2日の手紙で、モンゴメリに愛を告白している。二人の結婚に家族は反対であった。なぜなら、エドは鼻持ちならないシンプソン家の出身であり、モンゴメリとは、はとこ関係にあり、宗派が違っていたからである。エドはバプテスト派であり、当時、その宗派とモンゴメリの属する長老派との結婚は、容易に認められることではなかった。
　しかし、モンゴメリは、その後6月6日にエドを愛せると確

信し、6月8日には彼と婚約した。しかし、6月17日にはエドの抱擁に嫌悪感を感じ、婚約から10日ほどで、みずからのあやまちに気づくのであった。エドは一見非のうちどころのない、理想的な相手であった。しかし、努力はしたもののモンゴメリはいちばん肝心な愛を彼に感じることができなかったのである。そして、婚約した最初の週にエドを愛することをやめた——というよりむしろ、愛していたと想像するのをやめたのであった。1898年1月22日のモンゴメリの日記には、エドとのみじめな婚約の一部始終が告白されている。彼女は相手を傷つける結果になったことに心を痛めながらも、なんとかエドとの婚約を解消しようとする。しかし、プライドの高いエドは婚約破棄を認めず、なんとかモンゴメリを自分につなぎ止めようとする。彼女は長い苦悩と苦闘の末、やっとエドの束縛から自由になるのである。

　1897年7月1日、モンゴメリは仕事がきついうえに、土地柄も好きになれなかったベルモントを去り、一度家に帰った後、秋からロウア・ベデック（Lower Bedeque）の学校に就職する。

ロウア・ベデックの学校での教師時代
——ハーマン・リアードとの激しい恋

　運命の皮肉というべきか、ベデックの学校に得た代用教員の職は、エドの紹介であった。エドの友人アル・リアードが師範学校に戻って上級の教員免許取得のために勉強する間、代用教員を必要としたのであった。ここから人生の歯車が狂い出し、モンゴメリの精神的苦悩が始まるのであった。

　　去年の秋の夕方、湾を渡ってベデックへ行く途中、紫色の水平線に沈む赤々と輝く太陽や、遠くの岸の空にかかる

うす紫色の夕闇を無為に見ていた。将来のことがわかっていたなら、そのとき、その場で引き返し、それ以上遠くへは行かなかっただろう——そうすれば、たくさんの熱い涙や苦しい心痛、何日もの眠れぬ夜や激しい後悔を経験しなくてすんだだろうに。

　If I had known, that evening last fall when I crossed the bay to Bedeque and idly watched the great burnished disk of the sun sink below the violet rim of the water, and the purple shadows clustering over distant shores what was before me I think I would have turned then and there and gone no further——and thus I would have saved myself many a burning tear and bitter heartache, many a sleepless night and wild regret.（SJ 1898.4.8）

◇モンゴメリ24歳のころ。

　ベデックでモンゴメリは、アル・リアードの家に下宿する。アルの二人の弟のうち、彼女はハーマン（Herman）に魅力を感じる。彼は黒髪に、青い瞳、女の子と同じくらい長くつややかなまつ毛をしていた。27歳くらいだが年より若く見え、少年ぽかった。知性や教養のかけらもなく、農場や若者のサークル以外にはこれといった興味のない、いってみれば、素敵な若

い獣にしかすぎない若者であった。前述したモンゴメリの理想の男性像からはひどくかけ離れた人物であり、「ハーマン・リアードを夫として見る事はできなかった。このような男との結婚を夢見るのは、まったく狂気の沙汰」(Herman Leard was impossible, viewed as a husband. It would be the rankest folly to dream of marrying such a man. SJ 1898.4.8) と彼女は日記の中に述べている。それなのに、モンゴメリとハーマンは次第に親しくなっていく。

　ハーマンと出かけたバプテスト青年会の三度目の会合の折、モンゴメリは情熱と苦悩の小道への第一歩を踏み出したのであった。馬車で家に帰る途中、ハーマンはモンゴメリの顔を彼の肩に引き寄せた。彼女はそれを拒絶しようとするが、まるで魔法にかかってしまったようにそれに抵抗することができなかった。その後も、二人の関係は徐々にエスカレートし、その度にモンゴメリは、そのようなことを続けてはいけないと自己反省する。しかし、結果はいつも同じで、彼女は夜毎、ハーマンの愛撫に身を任せてしまうのである。

　　日々はまるで夢のように移り過ぎていくようだった。**生きている**と言えるのは、ハーマンといっしょの時だけ。あとの時間は、相反する情熱に苦しめられ、私の生活はついには長い苦痛となり、眠られぬ夜が健康にこたえはじめた。しかし、ハーマンの手か唇がひとたび私に触れるや、他のすべての感覚は、手放しの幸福にとけ合ってしまうのだった。

　The days seemed to me to come and go as in a dream. The only hours I *lived* were when I was with Herman. The rest of the time I was torn by conflicting passions until my life was one long agony and my sleepless nights began to tell on my health. But once let Herman's hands or lips touch mine and every other feeling was fused into one of unquestioning happiness. (SJ 1898.4.8)

　そして、事態はモンゴメリにとって「狂気」と思われるレベルにまで発展して行く。

　私はハーマンの激しい息を顔に、燃えるようなキスを唇に感じた。それから、彼が以前したのと同じ申出を私は聞いた。あからさまではなく、なかば聞取れないが、まちがいようのない申し出を。一瞬、それは一年くらいにも感じられたのだが、私の全存在はバランスを失った。もっとも恐ろしい誘惑が私をおそった——今でもその非常な力を覚えている——彼をここに留まらせ——せめてその夜、彼に身も心も**まかせたい**という誘惑である。

　I felt Herman's burning breath on my face, his burning kisses on my lips. And then I heard him making the same request he had made before, veiled, half inaudible, but unmistakable. For a moment that seemed like a year my whole life reeled in the balance. The most horrible temptation swept over me——I remember to this minute its awful power——to *yield*——to let him stay where he was——to be his body and soul if that one night at least!　(SJ 1898.4.8)

理性と感情の相克

　モンゴメリは二人の男性をめぐる恋愛のシーンでも、彼女に流れる二つの相反する血——情熱的なモンゴメリ家の血筋と清教徒マクニール家の良心——に翻弄された。

　　私には、とてもやっかいな気質が交じり合っている——情熱的なモンゴメリ家の血筋と清教徒マクニール家の良心。どちらも片方を抑制するほど強くはなかった。清教徒の良心でも激しい血気が思いのままに振る舞うのをやめさせることはできなかった——少なくとも、ある程度までは——しかし、それは楽しいことをすべて台なしにする可能性があり、実際にそうした。

　　I have a very uncomfortable blend in my make-up——the passionate Montgomery blood and the Puritan Macneill conscience. Neither is strong enough wholly to control the other. The Puritan conscience can't prevent the hot blood from having its way——in part at least——but it *can* poison all the pleasure and it does. (SJ 1898.4.8)

　また、これまで体験したことのない激しい恋は、モンゴメリの内面に長年育まれてきた他人を測る「ものさし」の目盛りまで狂わせてしまったようである。モンゴメリはたいへんプライドが高く、つねに自分の理想に照らして他人を判断する傾向があった。勿論、思慮深い彼女は、みずからの「ものさし」ではかった評価を口外することはけっしてなかった。彼女のこの性質は、老祖父母の名家の子女に相応しい気位と自尊心を持つようにという孫娘への厳しい躾に起因しているように思われる。

平生は理性的なモンゴメリも、やはり生身の人間である。理性が感情に屈しそうになることもあった。ベデックの下宿先でハーマンに出会ったとき、モンゴメリの「ものさし」は、もろくも目盛りが狂ってしまったのである。
　モンゴメリの心は、結婚したいが愛せない男性と、愛しているが結婚したくない男性の間で激しく動揺する。そんな折、モンゴメリ家とマクニール家の血が互いに争い、モンゴメリを苦しめるのであった。

　　情熱が「やれ！おまえの前に落ちてきた幸せのどんなかけらでもつかめ」と言う。良心は、「望むなら、そうしろ。おまえの魂に血のように真っ赤なイナゴ豆を食わせろ。だけどそのかどでのちにおまえを厳しく罰するだろう」と言う。

　　Passion says, "Go on. Take what crumbs of happiness fall in your way." Conscience says, "Do so if you will. Feed your soul on those blood-red husks; but I'll scourge you well for it afterwards." (SJ 1898.4.8)

　モンゴメリを「情熱」の誘惑から救ったのは、教育でも女性が払う代償の恐怖でもなかった。結局は、ハーマンから軽蔑されるに違いないという恐れが、モンゴメリに不名誉をもたらすハーマンの愛から彼女を救ったのであった。
　ハーマンとの燃えるような恋にもやがて終止符が打たれるときが訪れる。祖父が急死したため、モンゴメリは故郷キャヴェンディシュに戻り、祖母の面倒を見なければならなくなる。1898年4月2日、彼女はベデックをあとにした。

　　私は戸口の上がり段のところで、ハーマンにさよならを

言って、他の人と同じように握手をした。ハーマンは階段の踊り場に立って、私を見送ってくれた。すべてが終わった——私はこのまま人生も終わってくれればとだけ、せつに願っていた。

I bade him good-bye on the doorstep and shook hands with him as with the others. He stood on the platform and watched me off. It was all over — and I only longed and wished that life was over too!（SJ 1898.4.8）

帰郷——恋愛の後日談

　キャヴェンディシュへ戻ったモンゴメリは、ある日、1899年7月1日のパイオニア紙（*The Pioneer*）に前日死亡したハーマンの記事を見つけることになる。彼はインフルエンザの合併症で7週間病んだ後に亡くなった。

　モンゴメリの恋はハーマンの死をもって、終結した。彼女はこのことを日記に、「私の人生における最も痛ましい章の〈結末〉」（the "finish" to the most tragic chapter of my life; SJ 1899.7.24）と記している。彼女は、結婚できない相手ではあるが、亡くなったがゆえに、かえってハーマンを独占できることに安堵すら感じている。そこには愛する男性に対する女の恐ろしいまでの執念が見られる。

　　かつてまどろめぬ枕の上で、夜明けまで身悶えし、彼が私の愛にふさわしくないと胸が張り裂けんばかりに泣いた夜があった。だから、ハーマンが死んだ今、涙は必要なかった。私がかつて耐えた苦悩は何も匹敵するものはない。生きているときは決して私のものにはならなかったけど、

死んでいるハーマンの方が私のものと考えやすい。死んだらすべて私のもの。もはや他の女性が彼の胸にもたれたり、唇にキスしたりできないのだから。そういう意味で私のもの。

　There were once nights when I writhed on sleepless pillows until dawn and cried my passionate heart out because he was not worthy of my love. And so now, when he was dead, there was no need of tears for me. No agony could ever equal what I once endured. It is easier to think of him as dead, mine, *all* mine in death, as he never could be in life, mine when no other woman could ever lie on his heart or kiss his lips. (SJ 1899.7.24)

キャリアウーマン

　祖母の面倒を見る日々の中で、モンゴメリは1901年に半年ほどハリファックス（Halifax）のデイリー・エコー社で新聞の校正係り兼記者を勤めることになった。収入は充分といえないが、都会でさっそうと仕事にいそしむモンゴメリの姿を日記は描き出している。また、20世紀初頭のカナダにおける新聞社の様子や新聞の出来上がる工程がわかって興味深い。

　　私はザ・モーニング・クロニクル紙とデイリー・エコー紙のオフィスに一人でいる。新聞はもう印刷にまわり、追加の校正刷りはまだ来始めていない。階上では機械が回っていて、がたがたと不快な音をたて、アウアー・ライトの傘をひどく揺らしている。窓の外は、エンジンの排気ガスが猛烈に吹き出している。オフィスのなかではニュース編集者とユーモア・コラム担当者が激しく、親しく論争中。私――エコー紙の校正係り兼雑役係――がここに座っている。

前回の日記とはとてつもない「急激な変化」。私は新聞記者！

　I am here alone in the office of "The Morning Chronicle" and "Daily Echo". The paper has gone to press and the extra proofs have not yet begun to come down. Overhead they are rolling machines and making a diabolical noise which jars the shades on the Auer lights wildly. Outside of my window the engine exhaust is puffing furiously. In the inner office the news-editor and the "Beach-Comber" are having a friendly wrangle. And here sit I——*Echo* proof-reader and general handy-man. Quite a "presto change" from last entry. I am a newspaper woman!（SJ 1901.11.13）

祖母の面倒を見る日々

　祖母の面倒を叔父の長男プレスコットにいつまでも任せておくわけにはいかなかった。彼は祖母にとても意地悪く振る舞ったからだ。モンゴメリは気に入っていた新聞社の職をあきらめ、キャヴェンディシュに戻ることを決心した。

　祖母は次第に社交性を欠き、頑固になっていった。そんな祖母に隷属する単調な日々の中で、幼なじみは結婚し、遠くへ去って行った。モンゴメリは日記をつけたり、創作をしたりして自己実現の道を探っていた。交際をほとんど絶った生活の中で、文通は彼女にとって社会につながる窓であった。

　あるとき、モンゴメリの詩を雑誌で読んだ、自称作家を名乗るバージニアの男性が文通を申し込んできた。これがきっかけで、モンゴメリは何人かのペンフレンドを持つようになる。文通を通して彼らと文学や人生について意見を交換し合った。ア

ルバータのE. ウィーバー（Ephraim Wieber）とスコットランドのG.B. マクミラン（Geroge B. MacMillan）は、彼女の生涯を通じてよき文通相手となった。

4．『赤毛のアン』の成功──作家への道

『赤毛のアン』の創作

　作家への道は、けっして平坦なものではなかったが、モンゴメリは26歳になった1900年には、執筆でそこそこの収入を得始め、その翌年には、プリンス・エドワード島における主要若手作家の筆頭に挙げられるようになっていた。モンゴメリの処女作『赤毛のアン』は、1908年に刊行されたが、1907年8月の日記によると彼女はそのアイディアを3年前の1905年に得ている。日曜学校新聞の連載のために何かよい話の種はないかと創作ノートをめくるうちに、10年も前に記入した新聞記事からのメモ書きを見つけたのである。

　　　「老夫婦が孤児院に男の子を養子にほしいと申し込んだところ、まちがって女の子が送られてきた。」

　　　"Elderly couple apply to orphan asylum for a boy. By mistake a girl is sent them."（SJ 1907.8.16）

　これを読むうちに、モンゴメリの脳裏にある少女のイメージが浮かび、不思議なくらい彼女の心をとらえて離さなかった。そこで、この少女を主人公とする連載ものではなく、一冊の本を書くことにしたのだった。

　　　物語の基本的な構想と主人公はつかんでいる。あとはそれを一冊の本にするのに十分な数の章に引き延ばせばいいのだ。

You have the central idea and character. All you have to do is to spread it out over enough chapters to amount to a book.（SJ 1907.8.16）

　1905年5月のある晩から、一日の仕事が終わった後に書きためていき、翌年の1月に書き上がった。モンゴメリは自分の子ども時代の経験や「恋人の小径」など、キャヴェンディシュの景色をふんだんに散りばめて『赤毛のアン』を書き上げた。

『赤毛のアン』──ストーリー紹介

　もうすぐ11歳になるアン・シャーリーは、生後数か月にして両親と死別、以来他人の家を転々とし、4か月ほど前にホープタウンの孤児院へ送り込まれてきた。そして、スペンサー夫人の口ききで、まもなくプリンス・エドワード島のアヴォンリーへもらわれて行くところであった。

　そのころ、アヴォンリーにある「グリーン・ゲイブルズ（緑の切妻）」では、マシューとマリラ・カスバートという老兄妹が、10歳ぐらいの男の子を孤児院から引き取る心積りをしていた。齢を重ねたマシューに農作業の手伝いが必要だったからである。

　ところが、約束の日に駅に出迎えたマシューが目にしたのは、男の子ではなく、アン・シャーリーという女の子だった。濃い赤毛をした、そばかすだらけの痩せた少女を一目見るや、マリラは驚いた。翌日、さっそくスペンサー夫人を訪ねると、まったくの手違いであったことが判明した。折りしも手伝いの女の子を探しているブルウェット夫人のところにアンを回したらどうかという案も出たが、マリラは人使いの荒い夫人のもとへアンを送ることに気が進まず、結局、自分の手元に置いて育てることにした。

アンは快活で、おしゃべりで、想像力の豊かな子どもだった。アンにかかれば、ただのアオイの花も、サクラの木もボニーや雪の女王に変身してしまうのだった。しかし、アンは失敗も重ねた。自分を「赤毛」と呼んだ隣家のレイチェル夫人にひどい癇癪をおこしたり、「にんじん」とからかった学友ギルバートの頭を石版でたたいたり、牧師夫妻にふるまう菓子の香料を痛み止めの薬と間違えたり、行商人から買った毛染で、髪の毛を緑色に染めてしまったり……。一方、こうした事件の一つ一つが、老兄妹にこれまでの二人だけの暮らしでは味わえなかった生活のはりを与え、少女はいつしか、彼らにとって、掛替えのない存在となって行く。

　「恋人の小径」、「スミレの谷」、「輝く湖水」など、島の美しい自然に囲まれながら、アンはすくすくと成長していった。15歳になったとき、アンは教員免許取得のため、クィーン学院をめざして受験勉強を始めることになった。そして、奇しくも石版事件以来、張り合ってきたギルバートと同点のトップでクィーンに合格した。卒業間近には、奨学金を得てレドモンド大学へ進学できる道が開けていることを知った。アンの心は、将来の夢に膨らむのであった。

　アンは見事に奨学金を獲得した。同じくギルバートも。しかし、彼は学費を捻出する余裕が家庭にないため、地元で教員になる決心をした。秋にはレドモンドへ行くことになっているアンは、喜びに満ち溢れていたが、それも束の間であった。マシューの突然の死やマリラの目が不自由になったことが、アンの運命をすっかり変えてしまった。アンが大学へ進学した後、グリーン・ゲイブルズを売却するというマリラを、アンはアヴォンリーに残って教員になると言って説得する。事情を知ったギルバートは、地元の教職をアンに譲り、みずからはホワイト・サンズの学校に勤務することにした。アンは石版事件以来のい

がみ合いをすっかり水に流し、ギルバートと仲直りするのであった。

　アンの将来は、予想外に狭められてしまった。しかしアンは、けっして不幸ではなかった。真剣な仕事と、立派な望みと、厚い友情があり、なにものもアンが生まれつき持っている空想と、夢の国を奪うことはできないのだから。アンは「神、天にしろしめし、世はすべてこともなし」とささやくのであった。

『赤毛のアン』の出版

　モンゴメリの次なる課題は、出版社を探すことであった。彼女は原稿をまず、アメリカのインディアナポリスにあるボブズ＝メリル社へ送った。ここは何冊かのベストセラーを出して、急に有名になった出版社であった。モンゴメリは新進の出版社の方が新人に対して好意的であろうと読んだのであった。ところが、原稿はすぐに送り返されてきた。

　そこで次は前回とは反対に、大手の出版社、ニューヨークのマクミラン社へ原稿を送った。大手なら新人に関心を寄せる余裕があると目算したのである。しかし、今回も原稿は返送されてきた。

　そこで、今度はボストンにある中堅の出版社ロースロップ・リー・シェパード社を試してみた。結果はこれまでと同じであった。

　4度目は、ニューヨークのヘンリー・ホルト社へあたってみた。丁寧にタイプで打った返事がきたが、作品に対しては気のない褒めかたがしてあった。

　　　　物語には読者が「おもしろがる部分」もあるが、採用に足るほどではない。

> . . . their readers had found "some merit" in the story but "not enough to warrant its acceptance". (SJ 1907.8.16)

　これは、これまでに受け取った印刷してある不採用通知よりもひどくモンゴメリを傷つけた。
　返却された原稿は、そのまま古い帽子の箱に詰め込まれて、すっかり忘れられて一冬を越す。その後、モンゴメリはたまたま捜しものの最中にこの原稿を見つけだす。読み返してみると、なかなか面白かったので、もう一度出版社を試してみることにした。原稿の送り先は、ボストンのペイジ社であった。1907年4月15日、ペイジ社より4月8日付けの原稿採用通知が届いた。
　5度目の挑戦にして、『赤毛のアン』は、ついに出版に漕ぎ着けたのである。
　モンゴメリは苦労の末、『アン』の出版社を見つけたものの、その成功には確固たる自信がなかった。そこで、ペイジ社との印税は、卸値の10パーセントという、新人といえども不利な契約を結んでしまう。提示された印税率には不満があったが、出版が断られることを懸念して、ペイジ社に楯突けなかったのである。
　1908年6月20日のモンゴメリの『日記』を見ると、出版まもない『赤毛のアン』を手にした彼女の感動が伝わってくる。

> 　私の手のなかに、私の全存在の夢、望み、大志、苦闘の具体的な現実——私の最初の本がある。

> There in my hand lay the material realization of all the dreams and hopes and ambitions and struggles of my whole conscious existence——my first book! (SJ

1908.6.20）

　『日記』はさらに、モンゴメリが『赤毛のアン』の初版を手にしてから10日後に、すでにそれに対する書評が書かれ始めていることを明らかにしている。大方の書評は好意的であり、『赤毛のアン』が出版当初から高い評価を得ていたことがわかる。中でもモンゴメリをことのほか感激させたのは、イギリスの有力誌『スペクテイター』（The Spectator, 13 March, 1909）のNovelsの項目で、2段組とかなり紙面をさいて取り上げられたことであった。さらにモンゴメリを喜ばせたのは、アメリカ文学界の大御所マーク・トウェインからの賛辞であった（本書4頁参照）。

　一方、出版当初、『赤毛のアン』は児童文学というジャンルに限らず、フィクション（Fiction）、小説（Novel）等、さまざまなジャンルで取り上げられ、書評されている点は注目に値する。読者対象も、子どもから大人まで幅広い層に推薦しているものが多い。当時、アメリカでは「プロブレム・ノベル」（Problem Novel）と称される自殺、アルコール中毒、セックス等の社会問題を描いた大衆文学が蔓延していた。そうした状況のもとに、突如現れた健全で、清廉な作品として『赤毛のアン』は衆目をあつめたのである。大人の読者に支持されたからこそ、大成功したのである。

　カナダの片田舎を舞台にしたちっぽけな作品が、アメリカの大都会でベストセラーになるとは、モンゴメリ自身、想像だにしなかった。しかし、彼女が『赤毛のアン』の初版を手にしてから10日後に、すでに再版が出ている。そして刊行4か月後には、5版を重ね、名実ともにベストセラーとなった。

　モンゴメリの記録するところによると、『赤毛のアン』は出版初年度、カナダで775冊、オーストラリアで500冊、イギリ

スで500冊、アメリカで18,286冊、合計20,061冊売れている。翌年には倍増している。しかし、モンゴメリ自身は、当時情報が今日ほど発達していなかったせいであろう、隣国アメリカにおける自作の成功をそれ程実感してはいなかったようである。

　早くも1909年には、『赤毛のアン』の続編『アンの青春』（Anne of Avonlea）が出版されている。この作品では、16歳のアンがアヴォンリーの小学校の教師となって活躍する。隣人ハリソン氏の牛を自分のと間違えて売ってしまったり、若者たちと村の改善会を結成したり、双子を家に引き取って育てたり、中年の美しいミス・ラベンダーと彼女の昔の恋人で今は担任の生徒ポールの父親であるアービング氏とのキューピット役になったりして、楽しい日々を過ごす。やがて親友ダイアナはフレッドと婚約し、アンとギルバートは大学へ進学する。

ユーアン・マクドナルドとの結婚

　『赤毛のアン』は「幸せと希望を与えてくれる」作品（"the book radiates happiness and optimism" SJ 1908.10.5）として、評判は上々であった。しかし、当時のモンゴメリはこうした評価に首をかしげている。作品の明るさにひきかえ、作者の実生活はそれほどバラ色ではなかったからである。

　日々頑固になる老祖母に隷属し、社交を断った単調な生活は、やりきれないものだった。幼友達は結婚し、みんな去って行った。『赤毛のアン』は、実は、この孤独と精神的憂鬱の中で書かれていたのである。辛い日々に作家になる夢を追い続けることだけが、自己実現の道であった。そんな姿を作者はアンに投影しているのであろう。逆境にめげず向上心旺盛なアンは、モンゴメリの青春そのものである。辛い日々の中で、将来への一筋の光となったのは、ユーアン・マクドナルド（Ewan Macdonald）との出会いであった。

ユーアンはプリンス・エドワード島のヴァリーフィールドの出身であるが、その一族はスコットランドの高地人であった。彼は1903年9月にキャヴェンディシュ教会の牧師職に着任した。当時、ユーアンは中背で、がっしりした体格であり、容姿の良い、34歳位の若者であった。モンゴメリは「今は背筋が伸びて威厳があるが、いずれ、太鼓腹になるかもしれない」(. . . erect and dignified now, but may become "panchy" in later life. SJ 1906.10.12) と彼の印象を日記に記している。

　モンゴメリは最初、ユーアンに男性としてまったく興味をいだいていなかったし、魅力を感じていなかった。彼のことを大学教育を受けたにもかかわらず教養がないと見ていた。しかし、郵便物を出しに来るユーアンと話す機会が増え、彼のことをよく知るようになるにつれ、彼に期待していた以上のものを見つけるようになる。ユーアンがスコットランドへ留学する前に、モンゴメリは彼から求婚される。

　　　ぼくを最高に幸せにしてくれることが一つある。でも、多分、それは望みすぎだろうけど。それは君と人生を共にしたいということ——ぼくの妻になってください。

　　　"There is one thing that would make me perfectly happy but perhaps it is too much to hope for. It is that you should share my life——be my wife." (SJ 1906.10.12)

彼女は祖母が亡くなり、自由の身になるまで待ってくれるのならという条件で、婚約を承諾した。

結婚式から新婚旅行へ

　1911年3月、祖母がインフルエンザが原因で肺炎になり亡くなった。祖母から解放されたモンゴメリに、ユーアン・マクドナルドとの結婚の約束が実現される日がやってきた。祖母の死から4か月後の、1911年7月5日、二人は結婚した。
　『赤毛のアン』の続編『アンの夢の家』で、立派な若者に成長したアンとギルバートはめでたく結婚する。

　　その日、果樹園に囲まれたグリーン・ゲイブルズの家は、幸せにみちあふれていた。

　　Never had the old gray-green house among its enfolding orchards known a blither, merrier afternoon.
　　(*Anne's House of Dreams*, Ch. 4)

　モンゴメリはみずからの願望を作品世界で実現させたかったのであろう。彼女はアンのように白いドレスとベールに身を包み、白いバラとユリのブーケをかかえた花嫁となったが、自分が育った家で結婚式を挙げることはできなかった。そこは叔父が相続したからである。祖母の死後、住む家を失ったモンゴメリはプリンス・エドワード島のパークコーナーにある叔父キャンベルの家で式を挙げたのである。ここは、『銀の森のパット』(*Pat of Silver Bush*, 1933) の舞台であり、現在は博物館として一般公開されており、モンゴメリが結婚式を挙げた居間、ウエディングマーチが奏でられたオルガンなどが当時のままに保存されている。
　結婚式当日の正午、階下で賛美歌を歌う人々が待つ中、叔父に手をとられた花嫁は二階から階段を降りた。式は数分のうちに終わり、人々は「マクドナルド夫人」と彼女に声をかけた。

しかし、花嫁の心境は複雑であった。

　午前中私は満ち足りていた。落ち着いて、後悔の念もなく結婚式をとどこおりなく済ませ、祝福を受けた。式が終わり、ふと気が付くと夫の隣に座っていた——**私の夫**！——ふいに私は**反逆心**と**絶望感**に襲われたような気がした。**自由**になりたい！まるで、囚人のようだ——望みのないとらわれの身の。私の内なる何かが——激しく、自由で、おさえられない何か——ユーアンがおさえなかった——いえ、おさえられなかった何か——彼を主人として認めない何かが——私の枷となる束縛に対するある種の狂ったような抗議となってこみ上げてきた。その瞬間、もし結婚指輪をはずして自由になれるものなら、私はそうしたであろう、しかし、すでに遅すぎた——もう手遅れだという思いが不幸の黒雲となっておおいかぶさってきた。にぎやかな婚礼の宴、私はオレンジのつぼみの花冠と白いベールにつつまれ、私が結婚した男の隣席に座っていた——これまでの人生でもっとも不幸せであった。

　I had been feeling contented all the morning. I had gone through the ceremony and the congratulations unflustered and unregretful. And now, when it was all over and I found myself sitting there by my husband's side——*my husband*!——I felt a sudden horrible inrush of *rebellion* and *despair*. I *wanted to be free*! I felt like a prisoner——a hopeless prisoner. Something in me——something wild and free and untamed——something that Ewan had not tamed——could never tame——something that did not acknowledge him as master

——rose up in one frantic protest against the fetters which bound me. At that moment if I could have torn the wedding ring from my finger and so freed myself I would have done it! But it was too late——and the realization that it was too late fell over me like a black cloud of wretchedness. I sat at that gay bridal feast, in my white veil and orange blossoms, beside the man I had married——and I was as unhappy as I had ever been in my life.（SJ 1912.1.28）

　いとこのフリードが準備した祝宴のごちそうは素晴らしいものであった。だが、惨めな気持ちでいっぱいのモンゴメリは、食事が一口ものどを通らなかった。次に引用する幸福と自信に満ち溢れたアンとは違い、生身のモンゴメリには、結婚は必ずしもバラ色の人生を意味するものではなく、むしろ人生の墓場とうつったのである。

　けれども、その９月の正午、古い手織の絨毯を敷いた階段を降りてきたのは、幸せに満ちた美しい花嫁だった——グリーン・ゲイブルズの最初の花嫁。すらっとして、かすみのような花嫁のヴェールの奥で瞳を輝かせ、腕にはあふれるほどのバラをかかえていた。階下のホールで待っていたギルバートは、うっとりと花嫁を見上げた。とらえがたく、求め続けたアンがとうとう自分のものになったのだ。長い、忍耐の歳月の末に、勝ち得たアン。そのアンがついに降参して、すてきな花嫁として自分のもとにやってくるのだ。自分は彼女にふさわしい男だろうか。自分が望んでいるように彼女を幸福にできるだろうか。もしがっかりさせるようなことになったら——彼女の期待にかなう男にな

れなかったら——そのとき、アンが手を差し伸べると、二人の目が合い、疑念はすべて喜ばしい確信のうちに消えた。二人はたがいのものであり、どんな人生が待ちかまえていようとも、それを変えることはできないのだ。二人の幸せはたがいのうちにあるのだから、何も恐れるものはなかった。(『アンの夢の家』4章)

But it was a happy and beautiful bride who came down the old, homespun-carpeted stairs that September noon——the first bride of Green Gables, slender and shining-eyed, in the mist of her maiden veil, with her arms full of roses. Gilbert, waiting for her in that hall below, looked up at her with adoring eyes. She was his at last, this evasive, long-sought Anne, won after years of patient waiting. It was to him she was coming in the sweet surrender of the bride. Was he worthy of her? Could he make her as happy as he hoped? If he failed her——if he could not measure up to her standard of manhood——then, as she held out her hand, their eyes met and all doubt was swept away in a glad certainty. They belonged to each other; and, no matter what life might hold for them, it could never alter that. Their happiness was in each other's keeping and both were unafraid. (*Anne's House of Dreams*, Ch. 4)

『アンの夢の家』の中で、自分はそれに相応しい男だろうか。本当に彼女を幸福にする力があるか。もし期待するような男でなかったらというギルバートの独白は、実は祝宴の折り、隣に座っている夫に向けられたモンゴメリの自問ではなかったであ

ろうか。祝宴が終わるころ、モンゴメリは憂鬱な気持ちからどうにか立ち直り、新婚カップルはイギリスとスコットランドへと旅立っていったのであった。

　いまやモンゴメリは、一人前の作家となり、その年収は当時その地域で働く女性の20倍近くもあった。アンとは別の主人公が登場する『果樹園のセレナーデ』（Kilmeny of the Orchard, 1910）や『ストーリー・ガール』（The Story Girl, 1911）がこのころ書かれた。

　前者はモンゴメリの従来の作品とはひと味違う、ラブ・ストーリーである。果樹園に住む、バイオリンを弾く乙女キルメニイは絶世の美女であるが、口がきけない。しかし、代用教員エリック・マーシャルとの恋を通して、彼女は声を取り戻していく。そして、ついには、実は有名な会社の御曹司であったエリックとめでたく結婚する。

　『ストーリー・ガール』は、モンゴメリお気に入りの作品である。作中に二人のセアラが登場するため、ストーリーテリングにかけては天才の少女、セアラ・スタンリーの方は「ストーリー・ガール」とみんなから呼ばれていた。彼女こそ作者モンゴメリの分身にほかならない。

　売れっ子作家モンゴメリは嫁入り衣装として、新調したたくさんの服やブラウスや帽子を持って、2か月にわたる新婚旅行に出かけた。スコットランドでは、みずからのルーツを訪ねるとともに、ペンフレンドのマクミランと出会ったり、『ピーター・パン』（Peter Pan in Kensington Gardens, 1906）など若いころに読んだ名作ゆかりの地を訪問したりした。イギリスでは湖水地方をはじめブロンテ・カントリーとして知られるハワースを訪れている。ヨークでは大聖堂のそばの骨董品屋で陶器製の2匹の犬の置物を買っている。ロンドンからは祖母の育った家を訪ねるためにサフォーク州ダンウィッチまで足をのばした。

牧師の妻として、作家として

　新婚旅行から帰ると、二人はユーアンの新任地、オンタリオ州トロントから北東60マイルの郊外にあるリースクデール（Leaskdale）で新婚生活を始めた。海に囲まれ、開放的なプリンス・エドワード島に比べ、ここは内陸で一面に農地が広がる殺風景なところであった。

　しかし、リースクデールの15年間は、結婚、出産、育児とモンゴメリの人生においてもいちばん充実した時期であったので、おそらく自然の景観に不満を述べるひまはなかったと想像される。後に箱に詰められて送られてきたペットの猫のダフィーがいるだけで、プリンス・エドワード島はとても身近に感じられた。

　一方、トロントに近いことで、演劇を鑑賞したり、文学の集いに参加したり、島では味わえない都会の生活を満喫することもできた。

　当時の教会は、今日私たちが想像する以上に人々の社会や生活と密着していた。だから、牧師夫人にはコミュニティーの中心的役割が期待されていた。夫の補佐はもちろんのこと、日曜学校で子どもたちに教え、青年会では芝居の脚本を書いて演技指導を行い、さらに各信徒の家庭を訪問するなど、仕事は果てしなくあった。また、教区民から人生や家庭の悩みを打ち明けられることも少なくないが、牧師夫人はそれを聞くばかりで口外することはけっして許されない。モンゴメリは辛くなると、心の内を日記に吐露したものであった。

　1912年6月30日、モンゴメリのもとに新しい作品『アンの友達』（Chronicles of Avonlea, 1912）が届いた。アンの周辺にいる人々を主人公とした12話のオムニバスである。その中に、15年間もその愛をアンの友人セオドーラに告白できないでいるルードヴィック、今は亡きかつての恋人の娘にプレゼン

トを贈るロイド老淑女、愛し合っているのに15年間も互いに口をきかなかったリュシンダとロムニーなど、個性豊かな人々が登場する。

　この作品の評判も上々だった。こののちしばらくして、7月7日に長男チェスターが生まれた。モンゴメリは高齢出産を心配していたが、お産は案ずるより軽く、赤ん坊は健康そのものであった。おそらく、全身の筋肉を強化する体操と、お産を軽くする自己暗示の訓練が功を奏したのであろう。

　ところが、1914年二度目のお産は、まるで正反対であった。つわりがひどく、今回は女の子を望んでいたのだが、生まれてきた子はすでに死んでいた。へその緒がからまっていたのだ。何のために産まれてきたのかわからない息子ヒューの不条理な誕生に、モンゴメリは心を痛めた。折しも、第1次世界大戦が始まったというニュースをベッドの中で聞いたモンゴメリは、二重のショックを受けたのであった。イギリス連邦に属すカナダはいち早く義勇兵を送った。モンゴメリの身内でも異母弟カールが出兵し、片足を失った。

　1915年10月7日、三男スチュアートが無事誕生し、モンゴメリは悲しんでばかりもいられなくなった。彼女は牧師の妻として有能であったばかりでなく、家庭にあっても素晴らしい女性であった。料理や手芸が得意で、子どもたちには慈愛に満ちた母親であった。さらに驚くことは、モンゴメリが残した作品のほとんどは、結婚後の多忙な時期に書かれているのである。

　『アン』シリーズでは、『アンの友達』（*Chronicles of Avonlea*, 1912）に続き、『アンの愛情』（*Anne of the Island*, 1915）、『アンの夢の家』（*Anne's House of Dreams*, 1917）、『虹の谷のアン』（*Rainbow Valley*, 1919）、『アンの娘リラ』（*Rilla of Ingleside*, 1921）が出版された。以下、このシリーズを通して、18歳から54歳までのアンを追ってみよう。

5．アン、その後

『アンの愛情』

　ハリファックスをモデルにした町キングスポートにあるレドモンド大学にギルバートたちと進学したアン18歳の大学生活や恋愛が綴られている。アンは以前から気になっていた「パティの家」を借り、友達4人との共同生活が始まる。アンは「エイビリルのあがない」を書き上げ、雑誌社に送るが、どこからも採用されない。しかし、ダイアナがその原稿に手を加えたものが、モントリオールのローリング・リライアブル・ベーキングパウダー会社の宣伝用の懸賞小説に選ばれ、賞金を獲得する。純文学をめざしているアンはそれに落胆する。

　アンは普段から男子学生に人気があるが、20歳になったある早春の夜、ギルバートから求婚される。しかし、彼女はそれを断ってしまう。一方、金持ちで頭のよい、ヨーロッパ帰りの学生ロイヤル・ガードナーに「白馬の王子」を見いだす。大学卒業後、アンはロイから求婚されるが、彼が自分の結婚相手に相応しくないことをやっと悟る。その後、ギルバートは腸チフスにかかり死にかかるが、幸い病を克服する。アンは真実の愛に目覚め、ギルの再度の求婚を受け入れる。

『アンの夢の家』

　この作品ではアンとギルバートの新婚生活が描かれている。二人は結婚し、新居をフォア・ウィンズの「夢の家」に定める。そこでジム船長、ミス・コーネリア、レスリーといった人々との出会いがある。アンは甘い、幸せな新婚生活を送るが、生まれた赤ん坊のジョイスは一日も生きることなく亡くなってしまった。

　アンが海岸を散歩しているとき知り合ったレスリーは、18

年間も記憶喪失の夫ディックの看病をしていた。レスリーは、しばらく小説家のオーエン・フォードを下宿させるが、二人は互いに好意を持つようになる。医師のギルバートが、回復する可能性にかけて、ディックに新しい手術を施したところ、レスリーが夫ディックと思っていたのは、彼とうりふたつのいとこジョージ・ムアであることが判明する。ディックはキューバですでに亡くなっていた。というわけで、レスリーとオーエンは結婚できることになった。そして、アンとギルバートにはジェムというかわいい子が生まれた。二人は新しく、グレン村のモーガン邸を買い、引っ越していく。

『虹の谷のアン』

　アンの子どもたちにスポットがあてられる。アン夫妻がロンドンの医学会から帰ると、グレン村には新しい牧師が一家とともに赴任していた。彼はやもめで、4人の子どもがいた。子どもたちは、家政婦に面倒を見てもらっているものの、躾がなっていない。よく言えばのびのびと、悪く言えば野放図に育っていた。彼らはアンの子どもたちとすぐに仲良くなり、虹の谷に集まって遊ぶようになる。そこへメアリー・ヴァーンスというみなし子の家出少女が現れ、牧師館の子どもたちに助けられて、仲良くなっていく。およそ牧師の子どもに相応しくない行動の数々に、村人たちは、母親がいれば、彼らはもっとまともになるのではないかと考える。一方、読書家で夢想家の牧師は、やさしく素敵なローズマリーに出会うと恋に落ちて、結婚を申し込む。しかし、彼女は一生結婚しないという約束を姉とかわしていたために、牧師の求婚を断ってしまう。牧師館の子どもたちに畏れを成したローズマリーが、子育てに自信をなくし、牧師の求婚を断ったのだという噂を牧師の次女ユーナは耳にする。彼女は勇敢にも、父親と結婚してくれるようローズマリーに頼

みに行く。そして、二人はめでたく結ばれる。

　物語の最終部分でアンの長男ジェムが、クィーン学院に合格し、いずれおとずれる子どもたちの虹の谷からの巣立が暗示されている。

『アンの娘リラ』

　第1次世界大戦が始まると、50代になったアンはその末娘リラとともに銃後を守った。15歳のリラは初めてのパーティーに出かける。その最中に戦争のニュースが舞い込んできた。世界大戦は、ブライス家、グレン村、世界から明るさや楽しさを奪い去っていった。長男ジェムが軍隊に入隊し、リラは戦争孤児の赤ん坊を引き取って、育てる羽目になる。リラが思いを寄せるケニスもアンの次男ウォルターも入隊する。そして、後者は戦死。アンの三男シャーリーも入隊する。1918年、戦争勝利のニュースが届き、行方不明であったジェムが帰ってきた。リラが育ててきたジムスも父親の元へ引き取られた。ケニスは4年ぶりに炉辺荘で、一人前の女性に成長したリラと再会する。

新しい主人公——エミリー

　「アン・シリーズ」以外では、『ストーリー・ガール』（*The Story Girl*, 1911）の続編である『黄金の道』（*The Golden Road*）が1913年に出版された。ほかには詩集の『夜警』（*The Watchman and Other Poems*, 1916）、自伝である『険しい道』（*The Alpine Path*, 1917）が書かれている。さらに、モンゴメリはアンに劣らず魅力的な新しい主人公エミリー・バード・スターを創造し、『可愛いエミリー』（*Emily of New Moon*, 1923）、『エミリーはのぼる』（*Emily Climbs*, 1925）、『エミリーの求めるもの』（*Emily's Quest*, 1927）を著した。この3部作の中で、将来、作家を夢見る少女の成長が語られる。

メイウッドの窪地の小さな家に暮らしていたエミリーは、最愛の父を病気で亡くし、「ニュー・ムーン」(New Moon)に住む母方の古風なエリザベス叔母のもとに引き取られる。

　彼女は最初のうちは苦労するものの、新しい環境に次第に慣れ、イルザやローダといった友達を得ていく。エミリーの詩才を認める新任のカーペンター先生との出会いもあり、彼女は作家志望をますます強めていく。

　シュルーズベリーの高校へ進学したエミリーはその詩が活字になったり、芝居を演じたり、テディへの恋を感じたりと青春を謳歌する。高校卒業後は、彼女を気に入っている文芸記者ロイヤル女史の誘いで、ニューヨークの雑誌社で働くチャンスに恵まれる。しかし、エミリーはそれを断り、「ニュー・ムーン」に残る決心をする。

　帰郷したエミリーは、最初の本『夢を売る人』を書き上げ、複数の出版社に送るが、採用はかなわなかった。その後、彼女はディーンと婚約する。二人は新婚生活を送る「失望の家」の改装に多忙であったが、エミリーは本当に自分が愛しているのはテディであることに気づいていく。

　一方、テディは、エミリーが彼に関心がないものと誤解し、イルザと結婚することを決める。しかし、結婚式の当日、幼なじみのペリーの事故を知ったイルザは、ペリーへの愛を確信し、彼のもとへ走って結婚した。その後、エミリーはテディと結婚する。元の婚約者ディーンから彼女への結婚祝いは、「失望の家」であった。

　モンゴメリの日記が出版されて以来、アンよりもモンゴメリ自身の実像に近いという点から、近年『エミリー』3部作が注目されている。モンゴメリは日記の一部の清書と『エミリー』

の執筆を同時に進行していた時期があり、後者には、モンゴメリの実生活が色濃く反映されているのである。『可愛いエミリー』の結末で、エミリーは、彼女の死後に出版されるよう日記を書く決心をする。この一節は、モンゴメリの死後50年近くを経て出版された彼女の日記を暗示しており、興味深い。

書き続ける理由

　『エミリーの求めるもの』を除き、以上の作品はすべて、リースクデール時代に出版されたモンゴメリの作品である。

　アン・シリーズは、どれも成功したが、次々と続編を書くことに、モンゴメリはあまり気が進まなかった。もっと違うタイプの作品も書きたかったからである。一方、お金になるシリーズを止められない理由があった。夫ユーアンに憂鬱症の症状がはっきりと出てきたからである。モンゴメリは知らなかったのだが、彼は子どものころからこの病気の傾向があり、発作を繰り返してきたのだった。

　ユーアンは名医を求め医者を転々とするが、一点を見つめ、ふさぎこむばかりの夫を回復させる手だてはなかった。心身共に疲労困憊し、モンゴメリ自身も睡眠薬を常用する日々であった。万一、夫が職を失ったらと考えると、子どもの養育費のため、夫の治療代のため、モンゴメリはアン・シリーズを書き続けなければならなかったのである。

ノーヴァル

　1926年、モンゴメリ一家は、ユーアンの新しい赴任地である、トロントにさらに近いノーヴァル（Norval）という小村に移る。長老派とメソジスト派の統合をめぐるリースクデールのごたごたに、統合反対論者のユーアンが辟易した結果であった。

「ノーヴァルはオンタリオ州で美しい場所の一つと見なされいる」（Norval is considered one of the beauty spots of Ontario. SJ 1926.2.28）ところであった。子どもたちは、ときには頭痛の種をモンゴメリに与えながらも成長し、手がかからなくなっていた。執筆時間が充分とれるようになった彼女は、長年書きたかった大人向けの作品に挑戦し、『青い城』（*The Blue Castle*, 1926）と一種のミステリー『もつれた蜘蛛の巣』（*A Tangled Web*, 1931）を著す。

　前者はモンゴメリの作品の中でも特に自然描写が美しく、モンゴメリがめざしていた文学の理想の型をこの作品の中に垣間見ることができる。この作品を創作するインスピレーションをモンゴメリは、1922年に家族と共にムスコーカ湖付近のバラという避暑地を訪れた折りに得ている。この年は、ユーアンが前年におこした交通事故により、教区のピッカリング家から裁判に訴えられていたため、一家は遠出ができないという事情があった。現在、バラにはモンゴメリを偲ぶ博物館があり、毎年、「アンのそっくりさん大会」が開催されている。

バラと『青い城』

　『青い城』は美人でもなく、何の取り柄もなく、異性にももてず、家庭でも肩身の狭い思いをしてる29歳のオールド・ミス、ヴァランシーの恋物語である。医師から送られてきた診断結果で余命幾ばくもないと知った主人公は、余生を自分の自由意志で生きようと決心する。

　そこで近所の人々から秘密の過去を持つ悪漢と噂されている謎深い男性バーニー・スネイスに一方的に求婚し、結婚する。

　二人は自然豊かなムスコーカ湖の小島にあるバーニーの家で新婚生活を始めた。ヴァランシーはついに追い求めて

いた彼女の「青い城」を手に入れたのであった。『青ひげ』よろしく、夫には妻が聞いてはならない秘密がたくさんあった。しかし、未来のないヴァランシーは、夫の本当の職業さえ知ろうとしなかった。

　そのうちに、バーニーが有名な毛髪剤で成功した大富豪の息子であり、ヴァランシーの愛読書を著した作家ジョン・フォスターその人であることが判明する。一方、彼女の病気も、誤診であったことが医師から知らされる。無欲なヴァランシーは、百歳までも生きられるだろうという健康のお墨付きと今では彼女を心から愛する百万長者の御曹司の夫を手に入れたのであった。

モンゴメリはバラ滞在中に、かつての恩師マスタード先生の別荘を訪ねている。彼はモンゴメリが西部にいたころ、彼女に好意をよせていた高校教師である。その後、牧師となったマスタードは、若き日のモンゴメリの予想に反し、牧師として彼女の夫よりはずっと成功した人生を送っていた。

マリーゴールドとパット

　ノーヴァルでモンゴメリは『エミリーの求めるもの』（1927）を著し、エミリー・シリーズを完結させた。また、生まれてから4か月も名前が付けられなかった女の子の成長を12歳まで追った『マリーゴールドの魔法』（*Magic for Mariegold*, 1929）、家族が次々と家を去ったあと女主人となって屋敷を守っていく少女を描いた『銀の森のパット』（*Pat of Silver Bush*, 1933）を著した。

　このころ、1928年10月には、『アンをめぐる人々』（*Furhter Chronicles of Avonlea*, 1920）の出版トラブルや印税支払いに

関して10年越しに闘ってきたペイジ社との訴訟もようやく決着した。遡ること1917年7月、モンゴメリは『アンの夢の家』をそれまでのペイジ社ではなく、トロントのマックレランド・アンド・スチュワート社から出版した。これを不服としたペイジ社は、モンゴメリに支払う印税1000ドルの支払い拒否をしたのだった。女性は法に弱いと見くびっていた相手を裁判で正々堂々と打ちのめしてやったことに、モンゴメリは満足したのであった。

旅路の果て

> 1935年にモンゴメリは、『銀の森のパット』の続編『パットお嬢さん』(*Mistress Pat*)を出版する。この作品では、「銀の森屋敷」をこよなく愛するパットを中心に、11年の歳月が物語られる。その間、パットの周辺には彼女に思いを寄せる男性が複数現れ、パットはその中の一人と婚約する。しかし、銀の森屋敷に火災がおこり、焼け跡にたたずむとき、彼女が愛していたのは、幼なじみで建築家のヒラリーであることがわかる。二人はヒラリーが建築中の海のほとりの新居で新婚生活を始める。

これまで祖父の家や牧師館で暮らしてきたが、1935年、夫が退職したのを機に、モンゴメリはトロント市内にみずからの家を買った。ハンバー川に近いリバーサイド・ドライヴに建つチューダー様式を模したこの家は、モンゴメリの終の住み家に相応しく「旅路の果て荘」(Journey's End) と名付けられた。ここで彼女は、息子たちと再び一緒に暮らした。そして、この年、モンゴメリはオタワでジョージ5世より大英帝国勲位を受けた。またフランス芸術院会員にも選出されている。

「旅路の果て荘」で執筆された『丘の家のジェーン』（*Jane of Lantern Hill*, 1937）は、「家」探しの物語と呼んでもよい。この作品の主人公ジェーンの両親は離婚している。ある夏、彼女は父親と暮らすために、トロントからプリンス・エドワード島を訪れる。そこで親子は新しく買ったランタン丘に建つ家での生活を楽しむ。そのうちジェーンは、両親の離婚の原因を知る。その後、少女の病気を機に両親は互いの誤解を解き、一家は再び一緒に暮らすことになる。ジェーンは、両親とトロントで暮らすために購入したい家を冬の間に見つけていた。ハンバー川近くのレイクサイド・ガーデンズという通りにたたずむ家である。

『パットお嬢さん』の後、モンゴメリはしばらく休んでいた『アン』シリーズに再度、着手した。家の購入資金が必要だったからである。サマーサイドの中学校校長として過ごした日々が、婚約者ギルバートに宛てた手紙の形式で綴られている『アンの幸福』（*Anne of Windy Poplars*, 1936）は、『アンの愛情』と『アンの夢の家』の間に位置づけられる作品である。続く『炉辺荘のアン』（*Anne of Ingleside*, 1939）は、「夢の家」の後、「炉辺荘」に移ったアン一家の暮らしが語られている。話の中心は6人の子どもたちに移り、彼らの良き母親であるアンが、医師の夫に愛されながら、家族とともに生きる喜びを感じる姿が描かれている。

その後、モンゴメリは『ジェーン』の続編にも取り組むが、この作品が完成されることはなかった。

夫の病状の悪化、親の思い通りにならない息子に対する心労、第2次世界大戦勃発の恐怖などが引き金になり、彼女は心身ともに力尽きてしまったのであろう。もはや日記をつける気力さえ、沸かなかったようである。長年書き続けた日記の本格的な

記入は1939年6月30日で終わっている。

　モンゴメリは1942年4月24日、トロントで波瀾万丈の67年の生涯を終えた。死亡診断書によると、死因は冠状動脈血栓症とされている。彼女は、今、最愛の故郷プリンス・エドワード島に再び戻り、『アン』の舞台となったグリーン・ゲイブルズを見おろす墓地で、潮騒に抱かれながら静かに眠っている。

まとめ

　カナダの片田舎に生まれたモンゴメリは、幼いころから自分は周囲の子どもたちと違っていると感じていた。子ども時代から、自分はいずれ大したものになるという確信を持ち続けていた。この確信こそが作家という険しい道を歩むモンゴメリを支えていたように思える。彼女はまるで自己暗示にかかったように、成功をめざしてひたすら邁進した。もともと頭脳明晰、知性に溢れ、文才に恵まれたモンゴメリではあるが、一方、努力の人でもあった点も見落とせない。教師、新聞記者、どんな環境のもとでも、作家への自己鍛錬を怠らなかった。極寒の地カナダにあって、寒さで指先が青く変色しようとも、ペンを置くことなく、作家修業を続けた。

　　「ああ、大きな望みがあるのは、楽しいわ。こんなにもたくさん望みがあって、うれしいわ。限りがないみたいだけど、そこがいいのよね。一つの望みがかなうと、また別の望みがもっと高いところに輝いているんですもの。だから、人生って、とってもおもしろいのよね。」(『赤毛のアン』34章)

　　"Oh, it's delightful to have ambitions. I'm so glad

I have such a lot. And there never seems to be any end to them——that's the best of it. Just as soon as you attain to one ambition you see another one glittering higher up still. It does make life so interesting."
（*Anne of Green Gable*, Ch. 34）

というアンの言葉は、そのままモンゴメリの気持ちのあらわれであろう。
　モンゴメリは向学心に燃えた人でもあった。女性の高等教育が一般的でなかった時代に、チャンスを見つけては、教育を受け、実力を高めていった。その結果、モンゴメリの幼いころからの予感は、『赤毛のアン』の成功という形で成就したのである。
　モンゴメリの生涯を振り返ると、彼女は人間的にもひじょうにバランス感覚のとれた作家であることがわかる。主婦として、母親として、牧師の妻として家計を切り盛りし、子どもを教育し、信徒の世話をしながら25冊にも及ぶ著書を残したのであるから。モンゴメリの当時は、今日のように、家事の電化も進んでおらず、スーパーマーケットやコンビニエンス・ストアもなく、主婦にかかる家事負担は相当なものであったと想像される。しかも、彼女の死後発見された夥しい数のレース編みなどの手芸品は、モンゴメリが生活必需品の一部を手作りでまかなっていたことを示している。こうした生活環境の中で、彼女はどのようにして執筆の時間を捻出したのであろうか。モンゴメリは金銭面ばかりでなく、時間、仕事、家事など、万事において「やりくり上手」（economical）な人であったという印象を筆者は持っている。
　『赤毛のアン』執筆当時のモンゴメリの日記からは、彼女の抱く強い不安感や孤独感が読み取れる。しかし、読者は『ア

ン』から作者の実像を想像することは難しい。

　　ありがたいことに、私は自分の人生の陰の部分が作品に現れないようにすることができる。他人の人生を暗くしたくはない――それよりも、希望のメッセンジャー、喜びのもとでありたい。

　　Thank God, I can keep the shadows of my life out of my work. I would not wish to darken any other life ――I want instead to be a messenger of optimism and sunshine.（SJ 1908.10.15）

　ここに職業作家モンゴメリの真骨頂がある。モンゴメリは現実世界の辛さを彼女のぼやき帳でもある日記に吐露した。一方、理想や憧れや癒しの世界をみずからの作品の中に求めたのであろう。とくに結婚後、最愛のプリンス・エドワード島を離れ、そこに戻る家を失ったモンゴメリは、作品の中にこそ故郷を見い出すことができたのである。そして、それらは冊数を重ねるごとに、モンゴメリにとって小宇宙を形成していった。そこに一歩足を踏み込めば、故郷の懐かしい景色、心許せる人々、居心地の良い生活空間が広がっている。アンの家族やエミリーやパットやヴァランシーなど、個性豊かな主人公たちが息づいているのである。

　本書において、のちに詳しく紹介する香港からカナダへ移民したエイドリエン・クラークソン（Adrienne Clarkson）は、モンゴメリのこうした小宇宙を垣間見た一人であった。広大な新天地に親類縁者を持たない孤独な少女にとり、モンゴメリの主人公たちは、あまりにも生き生きとしていた。彼らは間もなく少女の肉親、カナダのいとこたちになっていったのである。

モンゴメリのファンは、みな、クラークソンのように、その小宇宙に魅せられた読者なのである。
　モンゴメリが生涯にわたって記録した克明な日記と彼女の作品は、表裏一体の関係にある。彼女の作品は、作家の実生活に基づいた日記に支えられているからこそ、説得力があり、百年のとき、洋の東西を越えて、多くの読者の支持と共感を得るのである。

II 作品小論

L.M. Montgomery

『赤毛のアン』は出版当初、子どもよりはアメリカの大人の読者の支持を受け、ベストセラーとなった。一方、1860〜70年代のアメリカでは、オルコット（Louisa May Alcott, 1832-88）の『若草物語』（*Little Women*, 1868）を代表とする少女向けのリアリスティックな作品が盛んに書かれていた。その後もクーリッジ（Susan Coolidge, 1845-1905）の『ケティが何をしたか』（*What Katy Did*, 1872）、ウィギン（Kate Douglas Wiggin, 1856-1923）の『少女レベッカ』（*Rebecca of sunnybrook Farm*, 1903）などの作品が続く。とくに後者は、主人公が未婚の叔母たちと暮らして、大人ばかりの家庭に新風をもたらし、夢見がちな少女から若い女性に成長していくストーリー展開が、『赤毛のアン』と酷似している。『赤毛のアン』は

◇『赤毛のアン』（*Anne of Green Gables*, 1908）の表紙。

いつしかアメリカの少女小説のジャンルに組み込まれていった。

そのような経緯から、『赤毛のアン』は伝統的には少女小説あるいは家庭小説として評価されてきた。しかし、最近はフェミニズム批評やカルチュラル・スタディーズの視点から『赤毛のアン』の新しい価値を探ろうとする動きが盛んである。ここではカナダ文学の視点から紙数の許す限り『赤毛のアン』の評価を試みてみたい。

『赤毛のアン』とカナダ的要素

大英帝国の植民地として出発し、アメリカ合衆国と隣接するカナダは、歴史的、文化的、経済的に二人のビッグ・ブラザーズに対して常にある種のコンプレックスを抱いてきた。カナダを代表する現代の作家であり、批評家であるマーガレット・アトウッド（Margaret Atwood, 1939- ）は、その著書『サバイバル』（*Survival*, 1972）の中で、優秀な二人の兄たちに対し、末息子カナダを敗者あるいは被害者ととらえている。彼女はカナダ文化のシンボルをアメリカの「フロンティア精神」、イギリスの「島」と比較し、「生き残ること（サバイバル）」と特徴づけている。

カナダが世界に誇る児童文学のジャンル「写実的動物物語」においても、アトウッドの指摘する特徴は顕著である。アーネスト・T. シートン（Ernest Thompson Seton, 1860-1946）やチャールズ・G.D. ロバーツ（Charles G.D. Roberts, 1860-1943）の描く動物物語は生き残るための闘いについて書かれており、そこに登場する野生動物は、天寿を全うすることはなく、やがて悲しい末路をたどる。アトウッドはこうした野生動物に、敗者あるいは弱者であるカナダの姿を重ねている。

『赤毛のアン』は往々にして少女小説や家庭小説と見なされるが、身寄りのない孤児が所属する家を求め、見知らぬ土地、

見知らぬコミュニティー、見知らぬ家庭に、幾多の困難を克服しながら順応していく様子は、単なる主人公の成長物語を超越している。まさに「サバイバル・ストーリー」(Survival Story)と呼んでも過言ではないであろう。この点で、『赤毛のアン』は充分カナダ的な作品なのである。

　一方、敗者が、あるいは弱者が生き延びたからこそ、名作になったカナダの作品も少なくない。たとえば、ロバーツの『レッド・フォックス』(*Red Fox,* 1905) は三代にわたる狐の大河ドラマであり、物語の最後で捕まえられ、狐狩り用にアメリカに売られた主人公のレッド・フォックスは、狩猟犬に八つ裂きにされるところを首尾よく脱出して、新天地を見つける。

　『赤毛のアン』は、主人公が大学進学をあきらめるため、最善の結末を迎えるとはいえないかもしれないが、養母の恩義に報い、長年のライバルを友人として認め、教師として自立しつつ、大学の勉学も独学で続けるという形で一種のハッピーエンドを迎える。

　アトウッドが指摘する「犠牲者」あるいは敗者としてのカナダ文学は、その結末を往々にして死や失敗に導きやすい。この点では、「サバイバル」に成功する『レッド・フォックス』や『赤毛のアン』は、特異な存在といえるかもしれない。

『赤毛のアン』の憂鬱

　アトウッドは『サバイバル』の中で、『赤毛のアン』の人気の一端を次のように分析している。

> 　カナダの作家の大半は、どんなに真剣さを装っていてもノイローゼ気味で病的である、ということかもしれない。そう決め込んで読者は、そういう本の代わりに『赤毛のアン』に没頭するかもしれない。(『サバイバル』お茶の水書

房、p. 33)

　You might decide at this point that most Canadian authors with any pretensions to seriousness are neurotic or morbid, and settle down instead for a good read with *Anne of Green Gables*. (*Survival*, p. 35)

　『赤毛のアン』が出版された折り、モンゴメリが彼女の作品に対する「幸せと希望を与えてくれる」という批評に対し、「『アン』を執筆していた当時の私の悩みや憂鬱や心配を考えると、本当にそうだろうかと思う」(When I think of the conditions of worry and gloom and care under which it was written I wonder at this. SJ 1908.10.15) と疑問を投げかけていることは、本書53頁において、すでに述べた。
　モンゴメリは明るく快活な少女を主人公とする『赤毛のアン』を、いくつかの精神的憂鬱の中で執筆していたのである。老人の世話に追われる日々は、激しい恋愛を経験した後にはことさら単調に感じられた。さらに不安もあった。モンゴメリが祖母と暮らす家は、祖父の遺言によりモンゴメリの叔父に譲られた。これは、祖母の死後モンゴメリは住む家を失うことを意味した。彼女は家を離れる寂しさに加え、この家以外で創作ができるのだろうかという不安に苛まれた。
　このように憂鬱な環境や精神状況にありながら、モンゴメリはそれを微塵も感じさせずに、『赤毛のアン』に象徴されるような、幸福で、読者に希望を与える文学世界の構築に成功したのである。ここに、『赤毛のアン』を単にカナダ的な作品から外国でも受け入れられる普遍的な作品へと昇華させた、モンゴメリの作家としての卓越した資質を見ることできる。

『赤毛のアン』の普遍性

　オックスフォード大学の数学教師ルイス・キャロル（Lewis Carroll, 1832-98）は、子どものための物語に教訓の必要がないことを直感で知っていた。その結果、彼の著書『不思議の国のアリス』（*Alice's Adventures in Wonderland*, 1865）は、近代ファンタジーの嚆矢となったのである。モンゴメリも児童文学の真髄を直感的に見抜くことのできた数少ない作家の一人であった。

　私は児童向けの作品を書くのが好きだが、もしその大部分に教訓を加えなくて良いのなら、もっと好きだろう。教訓無しでは児童書は売れない。私が書きたい児童書――さらに言えば、読みたい児童書は――活発で、愉快で、楽しいもの――「芸術のための芸術」――あるいは、むしろ「楽しみのための楽しみ」――陰険な教訓がスプーン一杯のジャムのように忍ばされていないもの。しかし、「小さい人」に本を提供しようとする編集者たちは、まじめすぎるので、雑誌の性格にふさわしい教訓が多かれ少なかれ加えられなければならない。

　I like doing these but would like it better if I didn't have to lug a moral into most of them. They won't sell without it. The kind of juvenile story I like to write ――and read, too, for the matter of that――is a rattling good jolly one――"art for art's sake"――or rather "fun for fun's sake"――with no insidious moral hidden away in it like a spoonful of jam. But the editors who cater to the "young person" take themselves too seriously for that and so in the moral must go, broad or

narrow, as suits the fibre of the particular journal in
　　view.（SJ 1901.8.23）

　この引用は、20世紀に入ってからもカナダでは、児童書には一かけらの教訓がつきものであったことを示している。こうした状況のもとで、モンゴメリは『赤毛のアン』を執筆する際に、教訓や日曜学校の理念をあっさり捨ててしまったのである。このため、『赤毛のアン』はモンゴメリのそれまでの作品とは一線を画しており、時空を越えて愛読される性質を備えているのである。

『赤毛のアン』と日本

　『赤毛のアン』は世界中で愛読されているが、とくに日本において人気が高い。その人気の秘密について、戦後の日本社会や経済成長とのかかわりを考慮しながら考察したい。

　『赤毛のアン』は1952年に村岡花子の訳によって三笠書房から出版された。村岡はNHKのラジオ番組「子どもの新聞」を長年担当するなど、女性文化人として戦後の日本社会に影響力を持っていた。こうした翻訳者を得たことにより、『赤毛のアン』はたちまち注目された。そして、逆境を克服し幸福をみずから手に入れるその主人公は、戦後の混乱に耐える希望と勇気を日本の子どもたちに与える理想の少女として、親や教師に歓迎されたのである。

　1953（昭和28）年の全国学校図書館法の成立にともない、学校図書館は良書を数多く必要とした。かくして、世界名作全集の出版ブームがおこった。日本語に翻訳された最初のカナダ児童文学である『赤毛のアン』は、家庭物語の好例でもあり、こうした全集に収録されて、日本の児童文学の基本作品となっていった。

その後『赤毛のアン』の続編も短期間のうちに翻訳された。女性の一代記を好む日本女性の読書傾向と合致して、モンゴメリの作品は人気を博した。

　1953年、日本においてテレビの放送が開始された。50年代の終わりごろには、テレビが子どもの文化へ影響を及ぼし始めるようになる。同じころ「コミック文化」も発展し始め、人気マンガがテレビでアニメ化される道が開ける。1964年の東京オリンピックはテレビが普及するきっかけとなり、「すばらしい新世界」（brave new world）の準備が整った。『赤毛のアン』も例外ではなく、1977年にマンガ化され、1979年にはアニメ放送がなされた。その結果、『赤毛のアン』は年齢の低い子どもにも浸透した。

　1980年代には、『赤毛のアンの手作り絵本』（1980）に代表されるような、若い女性を対象とした『アン』の周辺出版物が増加した。日本人による『アン』にヒントを得た、料理や手芸関連の図書である。また、プリンス・エドワード島の写真集、旅行記なども多数出版され、経済の高度成長に支えられ、プリンス・エドワード島への旅行者も増加し、『アン』への関心がさらに高まった。

　1989年と90年に『アン』と続『アン』の映画が劇場公開され、アン・ブームが再燃した。90年には、北海道に『赤毛のアン』のテーマ・パークが開園し、91年にはカナダからやって来た『アン』のミュージカルが日本の8大都市で上演された。『赤毛のアン』の新しい翻訳も完訳され複数の出版社から出版された。『赤毛のアン』の村岡花子訳は、後半の一部が原作と異なっていたためである。

　文学へのフェミニステック・アプローチが盛んになるにつれ、フェミニズムの視点からの『赤毛のアン』の再評価も盛んになった。

1985年から、モンゴメリの日記が *The Selected Journals of L.M. Montgomery* としてカナダで出版され始めた。その邦訳の出版は『赤毛のアン』の読者にモンゴメリの生涯への新たな興味を呼び起こし、モンゴメリ作品の再評価が始まっている。

過去50年間、日本の読者は『赤毛のアン』を愛読し、アンの世界を体験してきた。『赤毛のアン』は子どもから大人まで、一般読者から学者まで、共通の興味をわかちあえる数少ない貴重な作品の一つである。

『赤毛のアン』──多文化社会のアイデンティティ

同じく移民国家である隣国のアメリカ合衆国が「メルティング・ポット」（melting pot／人種のるつぼ）と呼ばれるのに対し、カナダはしばしば、民族の「モザイク国家」（Mosaic Nation）と呼ばれてきた。現在カナダは、多文化主義（マルチカルチュラリズム）政策をとっている。国民それぞれの祖国の文化を尊重しつつ、カナダという一つの国にまとまろうとしているのである。この精神の背後には、文化や宗教の異なる他人を認めることこそ、世界平和につながるというカナダ人の理想がある。この姿勢を法律で認めたのがカナダ多文化主義法（The Canadian Multiculturalism Act）である。1988年7月22日、正式に交付された。

カナダの有名なテレビ・プロデューサーで、後にカナダ総督となったエイドリエン・クラークソン（Adrienne Clarkson, 1939-)は、『L.M. モンゴメリとカナダ文化』（*L.M. Montgomery and Canadian Culture*, 1999）に興味深い序言を寄せている。その中で彼女は、東洋人の子どもが『赤毛のアン』を通して、いかにカナダ人になっていったかという、みずからの体験を語っている。

クラークソンは1942年、3歳のときに香港からの難民として

カナダに移住してきた。ちょうどアンが旅行鞄一つを携えてブライト・リバー駅に降り立ったように、彼女の両親はスーツケース2個を持って、新天地にやって来たのだ。

クラークソンが『赤毛のアン』を読んだのは、9歳のときであったという。彼女にはマシューやマリラが、カナダそのものに映った。二人は抑制的で、静かで、厳格であるが、礼儀正しく、寛大で、環境に順応できる人である。独身の老兄妹は、孤児の出現で期せずして、養父母となり、家族以外の者から愛されたのである。寛大なマシューとマリラは、まさに移民を受け入れるカナダと重ねることができる。

クラークソンは、モンゴメリの描くプリンス・エドワード島の島民を、新天地における彼女の親族と見なした。

彼女はモンゴメリの作品を通してカナダについて学び、カナダ人になっていったという。それはクラークソンにカナダの政治や宗教、価値観や帰属意識などを教えたのである。クラークソンの例は、『赤毛のアン』が建国期カナダの古めかしい作品ではなく、むしろ多文化主義を標榜する新しいカナダの子どもたちの求心力になることを示唆している。モンゴメリの作品は移民たちをその祖国を捨てずに、彼女の世界の一員にするフィクションの魔力を持っている。『赤毛のアン』は多文化社会のアイデンティティとして、これからもカナダの移民たちの「灯台の灯」となり続けることであろう。

Ⅲ 作品鑑賞

L.M. Montgomery

日記
(from *The Selected Journals of L.M. Montgomery*)

1

Cavendish, P.E. Island
Sept. 21, 1889

I am going to begin a new kind of diary. I have kept one of a kind for years—ever since I was a tot of nine. But I burned it to-day. It was so silly I was ashamed of it. And it was also very dull. I wrote in it religiously every day and told what kind of weather it was. Most of the time I hadn't much else to tell but I would have thought it a kind of crime not to write daily in it—nearly as bad as not say-

---

1
もうじき15歳になるモンゴメリは、この日から約50年間、日記を付けることになる。

1 **last but *not* least**「最後に大事なことを一つ言い残したが」
2 **handles**「名前、肩書き」
※この日の日記と『赤毛のアン』第4章の以下の記述を参照せよ。

"... What is the name of that geranium on the window-sill, please?"

"That's the apple-scented geranium."

"Oh, I don't mean that sort of a name. I mean just a name you gave it yourself. Didn't you give it a name? May I give it one then? May I call it—let me see—Bonny would do—may I call it Bonny while I'm here? Oh, do let me!"

"Goodness, I don't care. But where on earth is the sense of naming a geranium?"

"Oh, I like things to have handles even if they are only geraniums. It makes them seem more like people. How do you know but that it hurts a geranium's feelings just to be called a geranium and nothing else? You wouldn't like to be called nothing but a woman all the time. Yes, I shall call it Bonny. I named that cherry-tree outside my bedroom window this morning. I called it Snow Queen because it was so white. Of course, it won't always be in blossom, but one can imagine that it is, can't one?"

ing my prayers or washing my face.

 But I'm going to start out all over new and write only when I have something worth writing about. Life is beginning to get interesting for me—I will soon be fifteen—the last day of November. And in *this* journal I am never going to tell what kind of a day it is—unless the weather has something to do worth while. *And*—last but *not* least[1]—I am going to keep this book locked up!!

 To be sure, there isn't much to write about to-day. There wasn't any school, so I amused myself repotting all my geraniums. Dear things, how I love them! The "mother" of them all is a matronly old geranium called "Bonny." I got Bonny ages ago—it must be as much as two or three years—when I was up spending the winter with Aunt Emily in Malpeque. Maggie Abbott, a girl who lived there, had a little geranium slip in a can and when I came home she gave it to me. I called it Bonny—I like things to have handles[2] even if they are only geraniums—and I've loved it next to my cats. It has grown to be a great big plant with the cunningest little leaves with a curly brown stripe around them. And it blooms as if it *meant* it. I believe that old geranium has a soul!

2
Friday, April 8, 1898
Cavendish, P.E.I.
 ... I was very young at the time—barely twenty months old—but I remember it perfectly. It is *almost* my earliest

---

2
 この日の日記が示すように、記憶力の良かったモンゴメリは、2歳前に母と死別したときのことをよく記憶している。

recollection, clear cut and distinct. My mother was lying there in her coffin. My father was standing by her and holding me in his arms. I remember that I wore a little white dress of embroidered muslin and that father was crying. Women were seated around the room and I recall two in front of me on the sofa who were whispering to each other and looking pityingly at father and me. Behind them, the window was open and green hop vines were trailing across it, while their shadows danced over the floor in a square of sunshine.

　I looked down at the dead face of the mother whose love I was to miss so sorely and so often in after years. It was a sweet face, albeit worn and wasted by months of suffering. My mother had been beautiful and Death, so cruel in all else, had spared the delicate outline of feature, the long silken lashes brushing the hollow cheek, and the smooth masses of golden-brown hair.

　I did not feel any sorrow for I realized nothing of what it all meant. I was only vaguely troubled. Why was mother so still? And why was father crying? I reached down and laid my baby hand against mother's cheek. Even yet I can feel the peculiar coldness of that touch. The memory of it seems to link me with mother, somehow—the only remembrance I have of actual contact with my mother.

　Somebody in the room sobbed and said "Poor child!" I wondered if they meant me—and why? I put my arms about father's neck. He kissed me—I recall one more glance at the calm, unchanging face—and that is all. I remember no more of the girlish mother who has slept for twenty two years over in the old graveyard, lulled by the murmur of the sea.

3

Friday, March 21, 1901
Cavendish, P.E.I.

... I remember—who could ever forget it?—the very first commendation my writing ever received. I was about twelve years old and I had a stack of "poems" written out and hidden jealously from all eyes—for I was very sensitive about my scribblings and could not bear the thought of having them seen by those who would probably laugh at them. Even then I felt strongly, though inarticulately, that there was no one about me who understood or symphathized with my aspirations. I was not like the other children around and I imagine that the older people of my small world thought there was something uncanny about me. I would have died rather than show to them those foolish, precious little rhymes of mine.

Nevertheless, I wanted to know what others would think of them—not from vanity but from a strong desire to find out if an impartial judge could see any merit in them. So I employed a pardonable little ruse to find out. It all seems very funny and a little pitiful to me now; but then it seemed to me that I was at the bar of judgment for all time. It would be too much to say that, had the verdict been unfavorable, I would have forever surrendered my dreams. But they would certainly have been frosted for a time.

A school-teacher was boarding here then—Izzie Robinson. I liked her not and she liked not me. Had I shown her a "poem" and asked her opinion of it I would certainly have received no encouragement. But she was something of a singer and one evening I timidly asked her if she had

---

3
この日の日記が示すように、モンゴメリは12歳ごろに将来, 作家になることを決心した。

ever heard a song called "*Evening Dreams*". She certainly had not, for the said[3] *Evening Dreams* was a composition of my own which I then considered my finest effort. It is not now extant and I can remember the first two verses only. I suppose they were indelibly impressed on my memory by the fact that Miss R. asked me if I knew any words of the "song". Whereupon I, in a trembling voice, repeated the first two verses.

> "When the evening sun is setting
> Quietly in the west
> In a halo of rainbow glory,
> I sit me down to rest.
>
> I forget the present and future,
> I live over the past once more
> As I see before me crowding
> The beautiful days of yore[4]."

Strikingly original! Also, a child of twelve would have a long "past" to live over!

I finished up with a positive gasp, but Miss R. was busy sewing and did not notice my pallor and general shakiness. For I *was* pale—it was a moment of awful import to me. She placidly said that she had never heard the song but *that the words were very pretty.*

The fact that she was quite sincere must certainly detract from her reputation for literary discrimination. But to me it was the sweetest morsel of commendation that had ever fallen to my lot—or that *has* fallen since. Nothing has ever surpassed that delicious moment. I went out of the old

---

3   **the said**「上述の、上記の」
4   **yore** = [jɔː] 昔。

kitchen as if I trod on the amber air of the summer evening and danced down the lane under the birches in a frenzy of delight, hugging to my heart the remembrance of those words.

4

Wednesday, Dec. 3, 1903
Got a check for another serial to-day — the second I've sold. This has been a pretty good year for me in regard to literary work. I have attained a pretty firm foothold and have made $500 also. Editors often *ask* me for stories now; my name has been listed in several periodicals as one of the "well-known and popular" contributors for the coming year, and the Editor of the Pres. Board of Publication in Philadelphia wrote recently to ask for my autographed photo.

Yes, I *am* beginning to realize my dreams. And the dreams were sweeter than the realities. Yes, but the realities are quite decent, too. I enjoy my success for I've worked and thought hard for it. I have the satisfaction, too, of knowing that I've fought my own battles. I have never had any assistance and very little encouragement from anyone. My ambitions were laughed at or sneered at. The sneerers are very quiet now. The *dollars* have silenced them. But I have not forgotten their sneers. My own perseverance has won the fight for me in the face of all discouragements and I'm glad of it now.

4
この日の日記が示すように、モンゴメリは、やがて作家として成功することを予感していたのであろう。

5

Sunday, Mar. 26, 1905
Cavendish, P.E.I.

... In our sitting room there has always been a big bookcase used as a china cabinet. In each door is a large, oval glass, dimly reflecting the room. When I was very small each of my reflections in these glass doors were "real folks" to my imagination. The one in the left-hand door was *Katie Maurice*, the one in the right-hand *Lucy Gray*. Why I named them thus I cannot say. Wordsworth[5]'s ballad had no connection with the latter, because at that time I had never read it or heard of it. Indeed, I have no recollection of deliberately naming them at all. As far back as consciousness runs *Katie Maurice* and *Lucy Gray* lived in the fairy room behind the bookcase. *Katie* was a little girl like myself and

---

5

この日の日記にみられる〈本箱の友だち〉とよく似たエピソードは『赤毛のアン』第8章に登場する。以下、参照。

When I lived with Mrs. Thomas she had a bookcase in her sitting-room with glass doors. There weren't any books in it; Mrs. Thomas kept her best china and her preserves there—when she had any preserves to keep. One of the doors was broken. Mr. Thomas smashed it one night when he was slightly intoxicated. But the other was whole and I used to pretend that my reflection in it was another little girl who lived in it. I called her Katie Maurice, and we were very intimate. I used to talk to her by the hour, especially on Sunday, and tell her everything. Katie was the comfort and consolation of my life. We used to pretend that the bookcase was enchanted and that if I only knew the spell I could open the door and step right into the room where Katie Maurice lived, instead of into Mrs. Thomas' shelves of preserves and china. And then Katie Maurice would have taken me by the hand and led me out into a wonderful place, all flowers and sunshine and fairies, and we would have lived there happy for ever after. When I went to live with Mrs. Ham-

I loved her dearly. I would stand before that door and prattle to her for hours, giving and receiving confidences. In especial, I liked to do this at twilight when the fire had been lighted for the evening, and the room and its reflections were a glamor of light and shadow.

Lucy Gray was grown-up—and a *widow*! I did not like her as well as Katie. She was always sad and always had dismal stories of her troubles to relate to me; nevertheless, I always visited her scrupulously in turn, lest her feelings should be hurt, because she was jealous of *Katie*, who also disliked her. All this sounds like the veriest nonsense, but I cannot describe how real it was to me. I never passed through the room without a wave of my hand to *Kate* in the glass door at the other end.

━━━━━━━━━━━━━━━━━━━━━━━━━━━━━━━━

mond it just broke my heart to leave Katie Maurice. She felt it dreadfully, too, I know she did, for she was crying when she kissed me good-bye through the bookcase door. There was no bookcase at Mrs. Hammond's. But just up the river a little way from the house there was a long green valley, and the loveliest echo lived there. It echoed back every word you said, even if you didn't talk a bit loud. So I imagined that it was a little girl called Violetta and we were great friends and I loved her almost as well as I loved Katie Maurice—not quite, but almost, you know. The night before I went to the asylum I said good-bye to Violetta, and oh, her good-bye came back to me in such sad, sad tones. I had become so attached to her that I hadn't the heart to imagine a bosom friend at the asylum, even if there had been any scope for imagination.

5　**Wordsworth**　英国の湖水地方（the Lake District）に住み自然を歌ったWilliam Wordsworth（1770-1850）のこと。晩年は桂冠詩人（1843-50）となる。S.T. Coleridgeと共編の詩集である『抒情民謡集』（*Lyrical Ballads*, 1798）の出版を機に英国においてロマン主義が復興する。「ルーシー・グレー」（"Lucy Gray", 1800）はWordsworthの有名な抒情詩の一つ。

6

Friday, Aug. 16, 1907
Cavendish, P.E.I.

Here is a gap with a vengeance! But there has not been much to write about and I've been very busy and contented. Since spring came I haven't been dismal and life has been endurable and——by spells——pleasant.

One really important thing *has* come my way since my last entry[6]. On April 15th I received a letter from the L.C. Page Co. of Boston accepting the MS[7] of a book I had sent them and offering to publish it on a royalty basis!

All my life it has been my aim to write a book——a "real live" book. Of late years I have been thinking of it seriously but somehow it seemed such a big task I hadn't the courage to begin it. I have always hated *beginning* a story. When I get the first paragraph written I feel as though it were half done. To begin a *book* therefore seemed a quite enormous undertaking. Besides, I did not seen just how I could get time for it. I could not afford to take time from my regular work to write it.

I have always kept a notebook in which I jotted down, as they occurred to me, ideas for plots, incidents, characters and descriptions. Two years ago in the spring of 1905 I was looking over this notebook in search of some suitable idea for a short serial I wanted to write for a certain Sunday School paper and I found a faded entry, written ten years before : —— "Elderly couple apply to orphan asylum for a boy. By mistake a girl is sent them." I thought this would do. I began to block out chapters, devise incidents and "brood up" my heroine. Somehow or other she

---

6
この日記から『赤毛のアン』誕生の経緯が明らかになった。

6　**my last entry**「先日の記載」
7　MS＝manuscript

seemed very real to me and took possession of me to an unusual extent. Her personality appealed to me and I thought it rather a shame to waste her on an ephemeral little serial. Then the thought came, "Write a book about her. You have the central idea and character. All you have to do is to spread it out over enough chapters to amount to a book."

The result of this was "Anne of Green Gables".

I began the actual writing of it one evening in May and wrote most of it in the the evenings after my regular work was done, through that summer and autumn, finishing it, I think, sometime in January 1906. It was a labor of love. Nothing I have ever written gave me so much pleasure to write. I cast "moral" and "Sunday School" ideals to the winds[8] and made my "Anne" a real human girl. Many of my own childhood experiences and dreams were worked up into its chapters. Cavendish scenery supplied the background and *Lover's Lane*[9] figures very prominently. There is plenty of incident in it but after all it must stand or fall by "Anne". *She* is the book.

I typewrote it out on my old second-hand typewriter that never makes the capitals plain and won't print "w" at all. The next thing was to find a publisher. I sent it to the Bobbs-Merrill firm of Indianapolis. This was a new firm that had recently come to the front[10] with several "best sellers". I thought I might stand a better chance with a new firm than with an old established one which had already a preferred list of writers. Bobbs-Merrill very promptly sent it back with a formal printed slip of rejection. I had

---

8   cast ... to the winds 「あっさり捨ててしまう」
9   *Lover's Lane* 「恋人の小径」(モンゴメリは家畜の通り道をロマンティックにこう呼んだ)
10 come to the front 「有名になる」

a cry of disappointment. Then I went to the other extreme and sent it to the MacMillan Co. of New York, arguing that perhaps an "old established firm" might be more inclined to take a chance with a new writer. The MacMillan Co. likewise sent it back. I did not cry this time but sent it to Lothrop, Lee and Shepard of Boston, a sort of "betwixt and between[11]" firm. They sent it back. Then I sent it to the Henry Holt Co. of New York. *They* rejected it, but not with the formal printed slip of the others. They sent a typewritten screed stating that their readers had found "some merit" in the story but "not enough to warrant its acceptance". This "damning with faint praise" flattened me out as not even the printed slips could do. I put "Anne" away in an old hat box in the clothes room, resolving that some day when I had time I would cut her down to the seven chapters of my original idea and send her to the aforesaid Sunday School paper.

The MS lay in the hat box until one day last winter when I came across it during a rummage. I began turning over the sheets, reading a page here and there. Somehow, I found it rather interesting. Why shouldn't other people find it so? "Ill try once more," I said and I sent it to the L.C. Page Co.

They took it and asked me to write a sequel to it. The book may or may not sell well. I wrote it for love, not money — but very often such books are the most successful — just as everything in life that is born of true love is better than something constructed for mercenary ends.

I don't know what kind of a publisher I've got. I know absolutely nothing of the Page Co. They have given me a royalty of ten percent on the *wholesale* price, which is not generous even for a new writer, and they have bound me

---

11 betwixt and between 「中間の」

to give them all my books on the same terms for five years. I didn't altogether like this but I was afraid to protest, lest they might not take the book, and I am so anxious to get it before the public. It will be a start, even if it is no great success.

Well, I've written my book. The dream dreamed years ago in that old brown desk in school has come true at last after years of toil and struggle. And the realization is sweet —almost as sweet as the dream!

Ewan came home in April. He seemed very well and quite recovered from his headaches and insomnia.

7
Thursday, Oct. 15, 1908
Cavendish, P.E.I.

... One of the reviews says "the book radiates happiness and optimism". When I think of the conditions of worry and gloom and care under which it was written I wonder at this. Thank God, I can keep the shadows of my life out of my work. I would not wish to darken any other life— I want instead to be a messenger of optimism and sunshine.

7
　この日の記載は、モンゴメリが精神的苦悩の中で『赤毛のアン』を執筆していたことを示している。

創作

(from *Anne of Green Gables*)
CHAPTER III MARILLA CUTHBERT IS SURPRISED

 Marilla came briskly forward as Matthew opened the door. But when her eyes fell on the odd little figure in the stiff ugly dress, with the long braids of red hair and the eager, luminous eyes, she stopped short in amazement.
 "Matthew Cuthbert, who's that?" she ejaculated. "Where is the boy?"
 "There wasn't any boy," said Matthew wretchedly. "There was only *her*."
 He nodded at the child, remembering that he had never even asked her name.
 "No boy! But there *must* have been a boy," insisted Marilla. "We sent word to Mrs. Spencer to bring a boy."
 "Well, she didn't. She brought *her*. I asked the stationmaster. And I had to bring her home. She couldn't be left there, no matter where the mistake had come in."
 "Well, this is a pretty piece of business[1]!" ejaculated Marilla.
 During this dialogue the child had remained silent, her eyes roving from one to the other, all the animation fading out of her face. Suddenly she seemed to grasp the full meaning of what had been said. Dropping her precious carpet-bag she sprang forward a step and clasped her hands.
 "You don't want me!" she cried. "You don't want me because I'm not a boy! I might have expected it! Nobody ever did want me. I might have known it was all too beautiful to last. I might have known nobody really did want me. Oh, what shall I do? I'm going to burst into tears!"
 Burst into tears she did. Sitting down on a chair by the

---

1 **a pretty piece of business** business =「厄介なこと」

table, flinging her arms out upon it, and burying her face in them, she proceeded to cry stormily. Marilla and Matthew looked at each other deprecatingly across the stove. Neither of them knew what to say or do. Finally Marilla stepped lamely into the breach[2].

"Well, well, there's no need to cry so about it."

"Yes, there *is* need!" The child raised her head quickly, revealing a tear-stained face and trembling lips. "*You* would cry, too, if you were an orphan and had come to a place you thought was going to be home and found that they didn't want you because you weren't a boy. Oh, this is the most *tragical* thing that ever happened to me!"

Something like a reluctant smile, rather rusty from long disuse, mellowed Marilla's grim expression.

"Well, don't cry any more. We're not going to turn you out-of-doors to-night. You'll have to stay here until we investigate this affair. What's your name?"

The child hesitated for a moment.

"Will you please call me Cordelia[3]?" she said eagerly.

"*Call* you Cordelia? Is that your name?"

"No-o-o, it's not exactly my name, but I would love to be called Cordelia. It's such a perfectly elegant name."

"I don't know what on earth you mean. If Cordelia isn't your name, what is?"

"Anne Shirley," reluctantly faltered forth the owner of that name. "But—oh, please do call me Cordelia. It can't matter much to you what you call me if I'm only going to be here a little while, can it? And Anne is such an unromantic name."

"Unromantic fiddlesticks!" said the unsympathetic Mar-

---

2 **stepped lamely into the breach**　stepped into the breach「急場をしのぐ、難局の解決を図る」

3 **Cordelia**　コーディリア。Shakespeareの『リア王』(*King Lear*) に登場する王の末娘。三人姉妹のうちただ一人最後まで父王に孝行を尽くした。

illa. "Anne is a real good plain sensible name. You've no need to be ashamed of it."

"Oh, I'm not ashamed of it," explained Anne, "only I like Cordelia better. I've always imagined that my name was Cordelia——at least, I have of late years. When I was young I used to imagine it was Geraldine, but I like Cordelia better now. But if you call me Anne please call me Anne spelled with an e[4]."

"What difference does it make how it's spelled?" asked Marilla with another rusty smile as she picked up the teapot.

"Oh, it makes *such* a difference. It *looks* so much nicer. When you hear a name pronounced can't you always see it in your mind just as if it was printed out? I can; and A-n-n looks dreadful, but A-n-n-e looks so much more distinguished. If you'll only call me Anne spelled with an *e* I shall try to reconcile myself to not being called Cordelia."

"Very well, then, Anne spelled with an *e*, can you tell us how this mistake came to be made? We sent word to Mrs. Spencer to bring us a boy. Were there no boys at the asylum?"

"Oh, yes, there was an abundance of them. But Mrs. Spencer said *distinctly* you wanted a girl about eleven years old. And the matron said she thought I would do. You don't know how delighted I was. I couldn't sleep all last night for joy. Oh," she added reproachfully, turning to Matthew, "why didn't you tell me at the station that you didn't want

---

4　**But if you call me Anne please call me Anne spelled with an e.**　モンゴメリは母方の祖母の名をとってルーシー（Lucy）、ヴィクトリア女王の王女の名をとってモード（Maud）と名づけれられた。モンゴメリは 'e' をつけて 'Maude' と綴られるのを嫌った。'I was named Lucy after Grandmother and Maud after Queen Victoria's daughter, the Princess of Hesse, who died about that time I think. I never liked Lucy as a name. I always liked Maud——spelled *not* 'with an e' if you please——but I do *not* like it in connection with Montgomery.'（1911年5月23日のモンゴメリの日記より）

me and leave me there? If I hadn't seen the White Way of Delight and the Lake of Shining Waters it wouldn't be so hard."

"What on earth does she mean?" demanded Marilla, staring at Matthew.

"She — she's just referring to some conversation we had on the road," said Matthew hastily. "I'm going out to put the mare in, Marilla. Have tea ready when I come back."

"Did Mrs. Spencer bring anybody over besides you?" continued Marilla when Matthew had gone out.

"She brought Lily Jones for herself. Lily is only five years old and she is very beautiful. She had nut-brown hair. If I was very beautiful and had nut-brown hair would you keep me?"

"No. We want a boy to help Matthew on the farm. A girl would be of no use to us. Take off your hat. I'll lay it and your bag on the hall table."

Anne took off her hat meekly. Matthew came back presently and they sat down to supper. But Anne could not eat. In vain she nibbled at the bread and butter and pecked at the crab-apple preserve out of the little scallopped dish by her plate. She did not really make any headway at all.

"You're not eating anything," said Marilla sharply, eyeing her as if it were a serious shortcoming.

Anne sighed.

"I can't. I'm in the depths of despair. Can you eat when you are in the depths of despair?"

"I've never been in the depths of despair, so I can't say," responded Marilla.

"Weren't you? Well, did you ever try to *imagine* you were in the depths of despair?"

"No, I didn't."

"Then I don't think you can understand what it's like.

It's a very uncomfortable feeling indeed. When you try to eat a lump comes right up in your throat and you can't swallow anything, not even if it was a chocolate caramel. I had one chocolate caramel once two years ago and it was simply delicious. I've often dreamed since then that I had a lot of chocolate caramels but I always wake up just when I'm going to eat them. I do hope you won't be offended because I can't eat. Everything is extremely nice, but still I cannot eat."

"I guess she's tired," said Matthew, who hadn't spoken since his return from the barn. "Best put her to bed, Marilla."

Marilla had been wondering where Anne should be put to bed. She had prepared a couch in the kitchen chamber for the desired and expected boy. But, although it was neat and clean, it did not seem quite the thing to put a girl there somehow. But the spare room[5] was out of the question for such a stray waif, so there remained only the east gable room[6]. Marilla lighted a candle and told Anne to follow her, which Anne spiritlessly did, taking her hat and carpet-bag from the hall table as she passed. The hall was fearsomely clean; the little gable chamber in which she presently found herself seemed still cleaner.

Marilla set the candle on a three-legged, three-cornered table and turned down the bed-clothes.

"I suppose you have a nightgown?" she questioned.

Anne nodded.

"Yes, I have two. The matron of the asylum made them for me. They're fearfully skimpy. There is never enough to go around in an asylum, so things are always skimpy—at least in a poor asylum like ours. I hate skimpy night-

---

5　the spare room　来客用の予備の部屋。
6　the east gable room　東側の切妻屋根の下の部屋。

dresses. But one can dream just as well in them as in lovely trailing ones, with frills around the neck, that is one consolation."

"Well, undress as quick as you can and go to bed. I'll come back in a few minutes for the candle. I daren't trust you to put it out yourself. You'd likely set the place on fire."

When Marilla had gone Anne looked around her wistfully. The whitewashed walls were so painfully bare and staring that she thought they must ache over their own bareness. The floor was bare, too, except for a round braided mat in the middle such as Anne had never seen before. In one corner was the bed, a high, old-fashioned one, with four dark, low, turned posts. In the other corner was the aforesaid three-cornered table adorned with a fat red velvet pincushion hard enough to turn the point of the most adventurous pin. Above it hung a little six-by-eight mirror. Midway between table and bed was the window, with an icy white muslin frill over it, and opposite it was the wash-stand[7]. The whole apartment was of a rigidity not to be described in words, but which sent a shiver to the very marrow of Anne's bones. With a sob she hastily discarded her garments, put on the skimpy nightgown and sprang into bed, where she burrowed face downward into the pillow and pulled the clothes over her head. When Marilla came up for the light, various skimpy articles of raiment scattered most untidily over the floor and a certain tempestuous appearance of the bed were the only indications of any presence save her own.

She deliberately picked up Anne's clothes, placed them neatly on a prim yellow chair, and then, taking up the candle, went over to the bed.

7　the wash-stand（洗面器や水差しなどを載せる）洗面台。

"Good night," she said, a little awkwardly, but not unkindly.

Anne's white face and big eyes appeared over the bedclothes with a startling suddenness.

"How can you call it a *good* night when you know it must be the very worst night I've ever had?" she said reproachfully.

Then she dived down into invisibility again.

Marilla went slowly down to the kitchen and proceeded to wash the supper dishes. Matthew was smoking—a sure sign of perturbation of mind. He seldom smoked, for Marilla set her face against it as a filthy habit; but at certain times and seasons he felt driven to it and then Marilla winked at the practice, realizing that a mere man must have some vent for his emotions.

"Well, this is a pretty kettle of fish[8]," she said wrathfully. "This is what comes of sending word instead of going ourselves. Robert Spencer's folks have twisted that message somehow. One of us will have to drive over and see Mrs. Spencer to-morrow, that's certain. This girl will have to be sent back to the asylum."

"Yes, I suppose so," said Matthew reluctantly.

"You *suppose* so! Don't you know it?"

"Well now, she's a real nice little thing, Marilla. It's kind of a pity to send her back when she's so set on staying here."

"Matthew Cuthbert, you don't mean to say you think we ought to keep her!"

Marilla's astonishment could not have been greater if Matthew had expressed a predilection for standing on his head.

"Well now, no, I suppose not—not exactly," stammered

---

8 **a pretty kettle of fish**「困った事態」

Matthew, uncomfortably driven into a corner for his precise meaning. "I suppose——we could hardly be expected to keep her."

"I should say not. What good would she be to us?"

"We might be some good to her," said Matthew suddenly and unexpectedly.

"Matthew Cuthbert, I believe that child has bewitched you! I can see as plain as plain that you want to keep her."

"Well now, she's a real interesting little thing," persisted Matthew. "You should have heard her talk coming from the station."

"Oh, she can talk fast enough. I saw that at once. It's nothing in her favour, either. I don't like children who have so much to say. I don't want an orphan girl and if I did she isn't the style I'd pick out. There's something I don't understand about her. No, she's got to be despatched straightway back to where she came from."

"I could hire a French boy to help me," said Matthew, "and she'd be company for you."

"I'm not suffering for company," said Marilla shortly. "And I'm not going to keep her."

"Well now, it's just as you say, of course, Marilla," said Matthew, rising and putting his pipe away. "I'm going to bed."

To bed went Matthew. And to bed, when she had put her dishes away, went Marilla, frowning most resolutely. And up-stairs, in the east gable, a lonely, heart-hungry, friendless child cried herself to sleep.

CHAPTER XV A TEMPEST IN THE SCHOOL TEAPOT[1]

"What a splendid day!" said Anne, drawing a long breath. "Isn't it good just to be alive on a day like this? I pity the people who aren't born yet for missing it. They may have good days, of course, but they can never have this one. And it's splendider still to have such a lovely way to go to school by, isn't it?"

"It's a lot nicer than going round by the road; that is so dusty and hot," said Diana practically, peeping into her dinner basket and mentally calculating if the three juicy, toothsome raspberry tarts reposing there were divided among ten girls how many bites each girl would have.

The little girls of Avonlea school always pooled their lunches and to eat three raspberry tarts all alone or even to share them only with one's best chum would have forever and ever branded as "awful mean" the girl who did it. And yet, when the tarts were divided among ten girls you just got enough to tantalize you.

The way Anne and Diana went to school *was* a pretty one. Anne thought those walks to and from school with Diana couldn't be improved upon even by imagination. Going around by the main road would have been so unromantic; but to go by Lover's Lane and Willowmere and Violet Vale and the Birch Path was romantic, if ever anything was.

Lover's Lane opened out below the orchard at Green Gables and stretched far up into the woods to the end of the Cuthbert farm. It was the way by which the cows were taken to the back pasture and the wood hauled home in winter. Anne had named Lover's Lane before she had been a month at Green Gables.

1　**A TEMPEST IN THE SCOOL TEAPOT** cf. a tempest in a teapot 「ティーポットの中の嵐」、から騒ぎ。

"Not that lovers ever really walk there," she explained to Marilla, "but Diana and I are reading a perfectly magnificent book and there's a Lover's Lane in it. So we want to have one, too. And it's a very pretty name, don't you think? So romantic! We can imagine the lovers into it, you know. I like that lane because you can think out loud there without people calling you crazy."

Anne, starting out alone in the morning, went down Lover's Lane as far as the brook. Here Diana met her, and the two little girls went on up the lane under the leafy arch of maples— "maples are such sociable trees," said Anne, "they're always rustling and whispering to you," — until they came to a rustic bridge. Then they left the lane and walked through Mr. Barry's back field and past Willowmere. Beyond Willowmere came Violet Vale—a little green dimple in the shadow of Mr. Andrew Bell's big woods. "Of course there are no violets there now," Anne told Marilla, "but Diana says there are millions of them in spring. Oh, Marilla, can't you just imagine you see them? It actually takes away my breath. I named it Violet Vale. Diana says she never saw the beat of me for hitting on fancy names for places. It's nice to be clever at something, isn't it? But Diana named the Birch Path. She wanted to, so I let her; but I'm sure I could have found something more poetical than plain Birch Path. Anybody can think of a name like that. But the Birch Path is one of the prettiest places in the world, Marilla."

It was. Other people besides Anne thought so when they stumbled on it. It was a little narrow, twisting path, winding down over a long hill straight through Mr. Bell's woods, where the light came down sifted through so many emerald screens that it was as flawless as the heart of a diamond. It was fringed in all its length with slim young birches, white-stemmed and lissom-boughed; ferns and starflowers and wild lilies-of-the-valley and scarlet tufts of pigeon-berries[2] grew thickly along it. And always there was a delightful spiciness in the air and music of bird calls and the murmur and laugh of wood winds in the trees overhead. Now and then you might see a rabbit skipping across the road if you were quiet—which, with Anne and Diana, happened about once in a blue moon[3]. Down in the valley the path came out to the main road and then it was just up the spruce hill to the school.

The Avonlea school was a white-washed building low in the eaves and wide in the windows, furnished inside with comfortable, substantial, old-fashioned desks that opened and shut, and were carved all over their lids with the initials and hieroglyphics of three generations of school-children. The schoolhouse was set back from the road and behind it was a dusky fir wood and a brook where all the children put their bottles of milk[4] in the morning to keep cool and sweet until dinner hour.

Marilla had seen Anne start off to school on the first day of September with many secret misgivings. Anne was such an odd girl. How would she get on with the other children? And how on earth would she ever manage to hold her tongue during school hours?

Things went better than Marilla feared, however. Anne came home that evening in high spirits.

"I think I'm going to like school here," she announced.

━━━━・━━━━・━━━━・━━━━・━━━━・━━━

2 **pigeon-berries**「ヤマゴボウ」実は濃い紫色。
3 **once in a blue moon**「めったにしか起きない」
4 **a brook where all the children put their bottles of milk** . . . 学校の近くに住んでいたモンゴメリは、昼食は家に帰って食べた。学校に弁当を持っていくのは彼女の憧れであった。'. . . But it did not seem half so interesting as taking lunch to school and eating it, sitting in groups on the playground or under the tree with a bottle of milk that had been kept cool and seet in the brook water.'（1919年1月7日のモンゴメリの日記より）

"I don't think much of the master[5], though. He's all the time curling his mustache and making eyes at Prissy Andrews. Prissy is grown-up, you know. She's sixteen and she's studying for the entrance examination into Queen's Academy[6] at Charlottetown next year. Tillie Boulter says the master is *dead gone*[7] on her. She's got a beautiful complexion and curly brown hair and she does it up so elegantly. She sits in the long seat at the back and he sits there too, most of the time—to explain her lessons, he says. But Ruby Gillis says she saw him writing something on her slate[8] and when Prissy read it she blushed as red as a beet and giggled; and Ruby Gillis says she doesn't believe it had anything to do with the lesson."

"Anne Shirley, don't let me hear you talking about your teacher it that way again," said Marilla sharply. "You don't go to school to criticize the master. I guess he can teach *you* something and it's your business to learn. And I want you to understand right off that you are not to come home telling tales about him. That is something I won't encourage. I hope you were a good girl."

"Indeed I was," said Anne comfortably. "It wasn't so hard as you might imagine, either. I sit with Diana. Our seat is right by the window and we can look down to the Lake of Shining Waters. There are a lot of nice girls in school and we had scrumptious fun playing at dinner time[9]. It's so nice to have a lot of little girls to play with. But of

---

5 the master　Mr. Phillips はプリンス・アルバートの学校の教師で、教え子のモンゴメリに熱をあげていたマスタード先生を連想させる。
6 Queen's Academy　モンゴメリが学んだシャーロットタウンにあるプリンス・オブ・ウェールズ・カレッジがモデル。
7 *dead gone* = infatuated
8 slate「石盤」粘板岩から採った薄石板に木枠をつけたもの。蝋石の石筆をつかって、それに文字や絵をかいた。現代のノートと鉛筆の代わりをしたもの。
9 at dinner time　'dinner' は昼食。

course I like Diana best and always will. I *adore* Diana. I'm dreadfully far behind the others. They're all in the fifth book and I'm only in the fourth. I feel that it's a kind of disgrace. But there's not one of them has such an imagination as I have and I soon found that out. We had reading and geography and Canadian History and dictation to-day. Mr. Phillips said my spelling was disgraceful and he held up my slate so that everybody could see it, marked all over. I felt so mortified, Marilla; he might have been politer to a stranger, I think. Ruby Gillis gave me an apple and Sophia Sloane lent me a lovely pink card with 'May I see you home?' on it. I'm to give it back to her tomorrow. And Tillie Boulter let me wear her bead ring all the afternoon. Can I have some of those pearl beads off the old pincushion in the garret to make myself a ring? And oh, Marilla, Jane Andrews told me that Minnie MacPherson told her that she heard Prissy Andrews tell Sara Gillis that I had a very pretty nose. Marilla, that is the first compliment I have ever had in my life and you can't imagine what a strange feeling it gave me. Marilla, have I really a pretty nose? I know you'll tell me the truth."

"Your nose is well enough," said Marilla shortly. Secretly she thought Anne's nose was a remarkably pretty one; but she had no intention of telling her so.

That was three weeks ago and all had gone smoothly so far. And now this crisp September morning, Anne and Diana were tripping blithely down the Birch Path, two of the happiest little girls in Avonlea.

"I guess Gilbert Blythe will be in school to-day," said Diana. "He's been visiting his cousins over in New Brunswick all summer and he only came home Saturday night. He's *aw'fly* handsome, Anne. And he teases the girls something terrible. He just torments our lives out."

Diana's voice indicated that she rather liked having her

life tormented out than not.

"Gilbert Blythe?" said Anne. "Isn't it his name that's written up on the porch wall with Julia Bell's and a big 'Take Notice' over them?"

"Yes," said Diana, tossing her head, "but I'm sure he doesn't like Julia Bell so very much. I've heard him say he studied the multiplication table by her freckles."

"Oh, don't speak about freckles to me," implored Anne. "It isn't delicate when I've got so many. But I do think that writing take-notices up on the wall about the boys and girls is the silliest ever. I should just like to see anybody dare to write my name up with a boy's. Not, of course," she hastened to add, "that anybody would."

Anne sighed. She didn't want her name written up. But it was a little humiliating to know that there was no danger of it.

"Nonsense," said Diana, whose black eyes and glossy tresses had played such havoc with the hearts of Avonlea schoolboys that her name figured on the porch walls in half a dozen take-notices. "It's only meant as a joke. And don't you be too sure your name won't ever be written up. Charlie Sloane is *dead gone* on you. He told his mother — his *mother*, mind you — that you were the smartest girl in school. That's better than being good-looking."

"No, it isn't," said Anne, feminine to the core. "I'd rather be pretty than clever. And I hate Charlie Sloane. I can't bear a boy with goggle eyes. If any one wrote my name up with his I'd *never* get over it, Diana Barry. But it *is* nice to keep head of your class."

"You'll have Gilbert in your class after this," said Diana, "and he's used to being head of his class, I can tell you. He's only in the fourth book although he's nearly fourteen. Four years ago his father was sick and had to go out to Alberta for his health and Gilbert went with him. They were there three years and Gil didn't go to school hardly any until they came back.[10] You won't find it so easy to keep head after this, Anne."

"I'm glad," said Anne quickly. "I couldn't really feel proud of keeping head of little boys and girls of just nine or ten. I got up yesterday spelling 'ebullition.' Josie Pye was head and mind you, she peeped in her book. Mr. Phillips didn't see her—he was looking at Prissy Andrews—but I did. I just swept her a look of freezing scorn and she got as red as a beet and spelled it wrong after all."

"Those Pye girls are cheats all round," said Diana indignantly, as they climbed the fence of the main road. "Gertie Pye actually went and put her milk bottle in my place in the brook yesterday. Did you ever? I don't speak to her now."

When Mr. Phillips was in the back of the room hearing Prissy Andrews' Latin Diana whispered to Anne:

"That's Gilbert Blythe sitting right across the aisle from you, Anne. Just look at him and see if you don't think he's handsome."

Anne looked accordingly. She had a good chance to do so, for the said Gilbert Blythe was absorbed in stealthily pinning the long yellow braid of Ruby Gillis, who sat in front of him, to the back of her seat. He was a tall boy with curly brown hair, roguish hazel eyes and a mouth twisted into a teasing smile. Presently Ruby Gillis started up to take a sum to the master; she fell back into her seat with a little shriek, believing that her hair was pulled out by

10 Gil didn't go to school hardly any until they came back. このエピソードはモンゴメリ自身の体験を反映している。モンゴメリは15歳のとき、再婚した父親と暮らすために西部のプリンス・アルバートへ赴く。そこで、よい教育を受けたいと期待していたが、現実は継母から子守や家事手伝いを強いられ、まともに学校に通うことができなかった。1891年3月28日のモンゴメリの日記参照。

the roots. Everybody looked at her and Mr.Phillips glared so sternly that Ruby began to cry. Gilbert had whisked the pin out of sight and was studying his history with the soberest face in the world; but when the commotion subsided he looked at Anne and winked with inexpressible drollery.

"I think your Gilbert Blythe *is* handsome," confided Anne to Diana, "but I think he's very bold. It isn't good manners to wink at a strange girl."

But it was not until the afternoon that things really began to happen.

Mr. Phillips was back in the corner explaining a problem in algebra to Prissy Andrews and the rest of the scholars were doing pretty much as they pleased, eating green apples, whispering, drawing pictures on their slates, and driving crickets, harnessed to strings, up and down the aisle. Gilbert Blythe was trying to make Anne Shirley look at him and failing utterly because Anne was at that moment totally oblivious, not only of the very existence of Gilbert Blythe, but of every other scholar in Avonlea school and of Avonlea school itself. With her chin propped on her hands and her eyes fixed on the blue glimpse of the Lake of Shining Waters that the west window afforded, she was far away in a gorgeous dreamland, hearing and seeing nothing save her own wonderful visions.

Gilbert Blythe wasn't used to putting himself out to make a girl look at him and meeting with failure. She *should* look at him, that red-haired Shirley girl with the little pointed chin and the big eyes that weren't like the eyes of any other girl in Avonlea school.

Gilbert reached across the aisle, picked up the end of Anne's long red braid, held it out at arm's length and said in a piercing whisper:

"Carrots! Carrots!"

Then Anne looked at him with a vengeance. She did more

than look. She sprang to her feet, her bright fancies fallen into cureless ruin. She flashed one indignant glance at Gilbert from eyes whose angry sparkle was swiftly quenched in equally angry tears.

"You mean, hateful boy!" she exclaimed passionately. "How dare you!"

And then—Thwack! Anne had brought her slate down on Gilbert's head and cracked it—slate, not head—clear across.

Avonlea school always enjoyed a scene. This was an especially enjoyable one. Everybody said, "Oh" in horrified delight. Diana gasped. Ruby Gillis, who was inclined to be hysterical, began to cry. Tommy Sloane let his team of crickets escape him altogether while he stared open-mouthed at the tableau.

Mr. Phillips stalked down the aisle and laid his hand heavily on Anne's shoulder.

"Anne Shirley, what does this mean?" he said angrily.

Anne returned no answer. It was asking too much of flesh and blood to expect her to tell before the whole school that she had been called "Carrots." Gilbert it was who spoke up stoutly.

"It was my fault, Mr. Phillips. I teased her."

Mr. Phillips paid no heed to Gilbert.

"I am sorry to see a pupil of mine displaying such a temper and such a vindictive spirit," he said in a solemn tone, as if the mere fact of being a pupil of his ought to root out all evil passions from the hearts of small, imperfect mortals. "Anne, go and stand on the platform in front of the blackboard for the rest of the afternoon."

Anne would have infinitely preferred a whipping to this punishment under which her sensitive spirit quivered as from a whiplash. With a white, set face she obeyed. Mr. Phillips took a chalk crayon and wrote on the blackboard above her head:

"Ann Shirley has a very bad temper. Ann Shirley must learn to control her temper," and then read it out loud so that even the primer class, who couldn't read writing, should understand it.

Anne stood there the rest of the afternoon with that legend above her. She did not cry or hang her head. Anger was still too hot in her heart for that and it sustained her amid all her agony of humiliation. With resentful eyes and passion-red cheeks she confronted alike Diana's sympathetic gaze and Charlie Sloane's indignant nods and Josie Pye's malicious smiles. As for Gilbert Blythe, she would not even look at him. She would *never* look at him again! She would never speak to him!!

When school was dismissed Anne marched out with her red head held high. Gilbert Blythe tried to intercept her at the porch door.

"I'm awful sorry I made fun of your hair, Anne," he whispered contritely. "Honest I am. Don't be mad for keeps now."

Anne swept by disdainfully, without look or sign of hearing. "Oh, how could you, Anne?" breathed Diana as they went down the road, half reproachfully, half admiringly. Diana felt that *she* could never have resisted Gilbert's plea.

"I shall never forgive Gilbert Blythe," said Anne firmly. "And Mr. Phillips spelled my name without an *e*, too. The iron has entered into my soul,[11] Diana."

Diana hadn't the least idea what Anne meant but she understood it was something terrible.

"You mustn't mind Gilbert making fun of your hair," she said soothingly. "Why, he makes fun of all the girls. He

---

11 **The iron has entered into my soul,**「魂の中に鉄がねじこまれた」聖書の成句、'The iron entered into his soul.'(詩編105番第18節)参照。「非常な苦悩を味わった」の意味。

laughs at mine because it's so black. He's called me a crow a dozen times; and I never heard him apologize for anything before, either."

"There's a great deal of difference between being called a crow and being called carrots," said Anne with dignity. "Gilbert Blythe has hurt my feelings *excruciatingly*, Diana."

It is possible the matter might have blown over without more excruciation if nothing else had happened. But when things begin to happen they are apt to keep on.

Avonlea scholars often spent noon hour picking gum[12] in Mr. Bell's spruce grove over the hill and across his big pasture field. From there they could keep an eye on Eben Wright's house, where the master boarded. When they saw Mr. Phillips emerging therefrom they ran for the schoolhouse; but the distance being about three times longer than Mr. Wright's lane they were very apt to arrive there, breathless and gasping, some three minutes too late.

On the following day Mr. Phillips was seized with one of his spasmodic fits of reform and announced before going home to dinner that he should expect to find all the scholars in their seats when he returned. Any one who came in late would be punished.

All the boys and some of the girls went to Mr. Bell's spruce grove as usual, fully intending to stay only long enough to "pick a chew." But spruce groves are seductive and yellow nuts of gum beguiling; they picked and loitered and strayed; and, as usual, the first thing that recalled them to a sense of the flight of time was Jimmy Glover shouting from the top of a patriarchal old spruce, "Master's coming."

The girls, who were on the ground, started first and managed to reach the schoolhouse in time but without a sec-

---

12　gum　「トウヒのガム」トウヒの樹脂。

ond to spare. The boys, who had to wriggle hastily down from the trees, were later; and Anne, who had not been picking gum at all but was wandering happily in the far end of the grove, waist deep among the bracken, singing softly to herself, with a wreath of rice lilies on her hair as if she were some wild divinity of the shadowy places, was latest of all. Anne could run like a deer, however; run she did with the impish result that she overtook the boys at the door and was swept into the schoolhouse among them just as Mr. Phillips was in the act of hanging up his hat.

Mr. Phillips' brief reforming energy was over; he didn't want the bother of punishing a dozen pupils; but it was necessary to do something to save his word, so he looked about for a scapegoat and found it in Anne, who had dropped into her seat, gasping for breath, with her forgotten lily wreath hanging askew over one ear and giving her a particularly rakish and dishevelled appearance.

"Anne Shirley, since you seem to be so fond of the boys' company we shall indulge your taste for it this afternoon," he said sarcastically. "Take those flowers out of your hair and sit with Gilbert Blythe."

The other boys snickered. Diana, turning pale with pity, plucked the wreath from Anne's hair and squeezed her hand. Anne stared at the master as if turned to stone.

"Did you hear what I said, Anne?" queried Mr. Phillips sternly.

"Yes, sir," said Anne slowly, "but I didn't suppose you really meant it."

"I assure you I did"—still with the sarcastic inflection which all the children, and Anne especially, hated. It flicked on the raw. "Obey me at once."

For a moment Anne looked as if she meant to disobey. Then, realizing that there was no help for it, she rose haughtily, stepped across the aisle, sat down beside Gilbert Blythe, and buried her face in her arms on the desk. Ruby Gillis, who got a glimpse of it as it went down, told the others going home from school that she'd "ackshually never seen anything like it—it was so white, with awful little red spots in it."

To Anne, this was the end of all things. It was bad enough to be singled out for punishment from among a dozen equally guilty ones; it was worse still to be sent to sit with a boy; but that that boy should be Gilbert Blythe was heaping insult on injury to a degree utterly unbearable. Anne felt that she could *not* bear it and it would be of no use to try. Her whole being seethed with shame and anger and humiliation.

At first the other scholars looked and whispered and giggled and nudged. But as Anne never lifted her head and as Gilbert worked fractions as if his whole soul was absorbed in them and them only, they soon returned to their own tasks and Anne was forgotten. When Mr. Phillips called the history class out Anne should have gone; but Anne did not move and Mr. Phillips, who had been writing some verses, "To Priscilla," before he called the class, was thinking about an obstinate rhyme still and never missed her. Once when nobody was looking Gilbert took from his desk a little pink candy heart with a gold motto on it, "You are Sweet," and slipped it under the curve of Anne's arm. Whereupon Anne arose, took the pink heart gingerly between the tips of her fingers, dropped it on the floor, ground it to powder beneath her heel, and resumed her position without deigning to bestow a glance on Gilbert.

When school went out Anne marched to her desk, ostentatiously took out everything therein, books and writing tablet, pen and ink, testament and arithmetic, and piled them neatly on her cracked slate.

"What are you taking all those things home for, Anne?"

Diana wanted to know, as soon as they were out on the road. She had not dared to ask the question before.

"I am not coming back to school any more," said Anne.

Diana gasped and stared at Anne to see if she meant it.

"Will Marilla let you stay home?" she asked.

"She'll have to," said Anne. "I'll *never* go to school to that man again."

"Oh, Anne!" Diana looked as if she were ready to cry. "I do think you're mean. What shall I do? Mr. Phillips will make me sit with that horrid Gertie Pye—I know he will, because she is sitting alone. Do come back, Anne."

"I'd do almost anything in the world for you, Diana," said Anne sadly. "I'd let myself be torn limb from limb if it would do you any good. But I can't do this, so please don't ask it. You harrow up my very soul."

"Just think of all the fun you will miss," mourned Diana. "We are going to build the loveliest new house down by the brook; and we'll be playing ball next week, and you've never played ball[13], Anne. It's tremenjusly exciting. And we're going to learn a new song—Jane Andrews is practising it up now; and Alice Andrews is going to bring a new Pansy book[14] next week and we're all going to read it out loud, chapter about, down by the brook. And you know you are so fond of reading out loud, Anne."

Nothing moved Anne in the least. Her mind was made up. She would not go to school to Mr. Phillips again; she

---

13　**you've never played ball**　We have been playing ball in school all the spring and such fun as we do have! A Good game of ball is just glorious. It isn't baseball — don't know that it has any particular name — just "ball", that's enough. （1890年6月5日のモンゴメリの日記より）

14　**a new Pansy book**　「パンジー」ことG.R. オールダー夫人（Mrs. G.R. Alder）による子どもの生活を描いた物語シリーズ。1876年から出版。ロウスロップ社から出版された31冊のパンジー・ブックスの後、オールダー夫人他によりウォード・ロック社より出版された73冊のパンジーのシリーズが続く。どれも伝道、禁酒、祈祷を勧めている。

told Marilla so when she got home.

"Nonsense," said Marilla.

"It isn't nonsense at all," said Anne, gazing at Marilla with solemn reproachful eyes. "Don't you understand, Marilla? I've been insulted."

"Insulted fiddlesticks! You'll go to school to-morrow as usual."

"Oh, no." Anne shook her head gently. "I'm not going back, Marilla. I'll learn my lessons at home and I'll be as good as I can be and hold my tongue all the time if it's possible at all. But I will not go back to school I assure you."

Marilla saw something remarkably like unyielding stubbornness looking out of Anne's small face. She understood that she would have trouble in overcoming it; but she resolved wisely to say nothing more just then.

"I'll run down and see Rachel about it this evening," she thought. "There's no use reasoning with Anne now. She's too worked up and I've an idea she can be awful stubborn when she takes the notion. Far as I can make out from her story, Mr. Phillips has been carrying matters with a rather high hand. But it would never do to say so to her. I'll just talk it over with Rachel. She's sent ten children to school so she ought to know something about it. She'll have heard the whole story, too, by this time."

Marilla found Mrs. Lynde knitting quilts as industriously and cheerfully as usual.

"I suppose you know what I've come about," she said, a little shamefacedly.

Mrs. Rachel nodded.

"About Anne's fuss in school, I reckon," she said. "Tillie Boulter was in on her way home from school and told me about it."

"I don't know what to do with her," said Marilla. "She

declares she won't go back to school. I never saw a child so worked up. I've been expecting trouble ever since she started to school. I knew things were going too smooth to last. She's so high-strung. What would you advise, Rachel?"

"Well, since you've asked my advice, Marilla," said Mrs. Lynde amiably——Mrs. Lynde dearly loved to be asked for advice——"I'd just humour her a little at first, that's what I'd do. It's my belief that Mr. Phillips was in the wrong. Of course, it doesn't do to say so to the children, you know. And of course he did right to punish her yesterday for giving way to temper. But to-day it was different. The others who were late should have been punished as well as Anne, that's what. And I don't believe in making the girls sit with the boys for punishment. It isn't modest. Tillie Boulter was real indignant. She took Anne's part right through and said all the scholars did, too. Anne seems real popular among them, somehow. I never thought she'd take with them so well."

"Then you really think I'd better let her stay home," said Marilla in amazement.

"Yes. That is, I wouldn't say school to her again until she said it herself. Depend upon it, Marilla, she'll cool off in a week or so and be ready enough to go back of her own accord, that's what, while, if you were to make her go back right off, dear knows what freak or tantrum she'd take next and make more trouble than ever. The less fuss made the better in my opinion. She won't miss much by not going to school, as far as *that* goes. Mr. Phillips isn't any good at all as a teacher. The order he keeps is scandalous, that's what and he neglects the young fry[15] and puts all his time on those big scholars he's getting ready for

---

15 the young fry 「子どもたち」シェイクスピアの『マクベス』'What you egg!／Young fry of treachery!' (4幕2場84〜5行) 参照。

Queen's. He'd never have got the school for another year if his uncle hadn't been a trustee—*the* trustee, for he just leads the other two around by the nose, that's what. I declare, I don't know what education in this Island is coming to."

Mrs. Rachel shook her head, as much as to say if she were only at the head of the educational system of the Province things would be much better managed.

Marilla took Mrs. Rachel's advice and not another word was said to Anne about going back to school. She learned her lessons at home, did her chores, and played with Diana in the chilly purple autumn twilights; but when she met Gilbert Blythe on the road or encountered him in Sunday School she passed him by with an icy contempt that was no whit thawed by his evident desire to appease her. Even Diana's efforts as peacemaker were of no avail. Anne had evidently made up her mind to hate Gilbert Blythe to the end of life.

As much as she hated Gilbert, however, did she love Diana, with all the love of her passionate little heart, equally intense in its likes and dislikes. One evening Marilla, coming in from the orchard with a basket of apples, found Anne sitting alone by the east window in the twilight, crying bitterly.

"Whatever's the matter now, Anne?" she asked.

"It's about Diana," sobbed Anne luxuriously. "I love Diana so, Marilla. I cannot ever live without her. But I know very well when we grow up that Diana will get married and go away and leave me. And oh, what shall I do? I hate her husband—I just hate him furiously. I've been imagining it all out—the wedding and everything—Diana dressed in snowy garments, with a veil, and looking as beautiful and regal as a queen; and me the bridesmaid, with a lovely dress, too, and puffed sleeves, but with a breaking heart hid beneath my smiling face. And then bidding Diana good-bye-e-e——" Here Anne broke down entirely and wept with increasing bitterness.

Marilla turned quickly away to hide her twitching face; but it was no use; she collapsed on the nearest chair and burst into such a hearty and unusual peal of laughter that Matthew, crossing the yard outside, halted in amazement. When had he heard Marilla laugh like that before?

"Well, Anne Shirley," said Marilla as soon as she could speak, "if you must borrow trouble, for pity's sake borrow it handier home. I should think you had an imagination, sure enough."

詩
(from *The Watchman and Other Poems*)
Before Storm

There's a grayness over the harbor like fear on the face of a woman,
    The sob of the waves has a sound akin to a woman's cry,
And the deeps beyond the bar are moaning with evil presage
    Of a storm that will leap from its lair in that dour north-eastern sky.

Slowly the pale mists rise, like ghosts of the sea, in the offing,
    Creeping all wan and chilly by headland and sunken reef,
And a wind is wailing and keening like a lost thing 'mid[1] the islands,
Boding of wreck and tempest, plaining of dolor and grief.

Swiftly the boats come homeward, over the grim bar crowding,
    Like birds that flee to their shelter in hurry and affright,
Only the wild gray gulls that love the cloud and the clamor
    Will dare to tempt the ways of the ravening sea to-night.

But the ship that sailed at the dawning, manned by the lads that love us
    God help and pity her when the storm is loosed on her track!
Oh women, we pray to-night and keep a vigil of sorrow
    For those we sped at the dawning and may never welcome back!

　海、海辺、森など自然はモンゴメリが好んだ詩のテーマである。本書にとりあげた2篇はモンゴメリの詩の選集 *The Poetry of Lucy Maud Montgomery* (Selected and Introduced by John Ferns and Kevin McCabe, Markham: Fitzhenry & Whiteside, 1987) にも収録されている。
　1　**mid**=amid

The Wood Pool

Here is a voice that soundeth[2] low and far
    And lyric—voice of wind among the pines,
Where the untroubled, glimmering waters are,
    And sunlight seldom shines.

Elusive shadows linger shyly here,
    And wood-flowers blow, like pale sweet spirit-bloom;
And white slim birches whisper, mirrored clear
    In the pool's lucent gloom.

Here Pan might pipe, or wandering dryad kneel
    To view her loveliness beside the brim,
Or laughing wood-nymphs from the byways steal
    To dance around its rim.

'Tis[3] such a witching spot as might beseem
    A seeker of young friendship's trysting-place,
Or lover yielding to the immortal dream
    Of one beloved face.

---

2   **soundeth** = sounds
3   **'Tis** = It is の短縮形

年表・参考文献

L.M. Montgomery

西暦年	年齢	事　項
1874	0	11月30日、プリンス・エドワード島のクリフトン、現在のニュー・ロンドンに誕生。父ヒュー・ジョン・モンゴメリと母クレアラ・ウルナー・マクニールの第一子。
1876	2	生後20か月で母と死別。その後、母方の祖父母にキャヴェンディシュで養育される。
1889	15	9月21日、現存する日記を書き始める。
1890	16	再婚した父と暮らすため、西部のプリンス・アルバートへ赴く。
1891	17	キャヴェンディシュに戻り、再び祖父母と暮らす。
1893	19	シャーロットタウンのプリンス・オブ・ウエールズ・カレッジに入学(教員免許コース)。
1894	20	PWC卒業。ビディファドの学校に着任。
1895	21	ビディファドの学校辞職。ダルハウジー大学で英文学のコース受講。
1896	22	ベルモントの学校で教鞭をとる。
1897	23	エド・シンプソンと婚約。ロウア・ベデックで代用教員となる。
1898	24	下宿先の息子ハーマン・リアードと恋愛。祖父死亡。祖母と暮らすため、キャヴェンディシュへ戻る。
1899	25	ハーマン死去。
1900	26	父、肺炎により死亡。
1901	27	ハリファックスのデイリー・エコー紙の校正係り兼記者となる。
1902	28	デイリー・エコー社辞職。アルバータ州に住むイーフレイム・ウィーバーと文通を始める。
1903	29	スコットランドに住むG.B.マクミランと文通を始める。
1905	31	『赤毛のアン』を書き始める。
1906	32	『赤毛のアン』の原稿を4社に送るが、すべて不採用。牧師ユーアン・マクドナルドと婚約。

西暦年	年齢	事　項
1907	33	ボストンのL.C. ペイジ社、『赤毛のアン』の出版を承諾。
1908	34	6月20日、『赤毛のアン』出版。
1909	35	『アンの青春』出版。
1911	37	3月、祖母死亡。7月5日、ユーアンと結婚。スコットランドへ新婚旅行の後、夫の赴任地オンタリオ州リースクデールの牧師館へ移る。
1912	38	『アンの友達』出版。長男チェスター誕生。
1914	40	次男ヒュー死産。
1915	41	三男スチュアート誕生。『アンの愛情』出版。
1917	43	『アンの夢の家』出版。自叙伝『険しい道』 *Everywoman's world* に掲載。
1919	45	『虹の谷のアン』 出版。『赤毛のアン』映画化。
1920	46	ペイジ社、著者の承諾を得ずに『アンをめぐる人々』出版。長年にわたる裁判の原因となる。
1921	47	『アンの娘リラ』 を執筆し、アン・シリーズを中断。
1923	49	『可愛いエミリー』 出版。
1925	51	『エミリーはのぼる』 出版。
1926	52	オンタリオ州ノーヴァルの牧師館へ移る。『青い城』出版。
1927	53	『エミリーの求めるもの』出版。
1935	61	退職した夫と共にトロントの「旅路の果て荘」に移り住む。大英帝国勲位を授与される。
1936	62	『アンの幸福』 出版。
1939	65	『炉辺荘のアン』 出版。
1942	68	4月24日、永眠。キャヴェンディシュの共同墓地に埋葬される。(1943 夫ユーアン死去。)

※年齢は誕生日以後の満年齢数。

【1】作品

　（☆印の作品は、McClelland-Bantam Inc. (Toronto) の'A Seal Book' というペーパーバックシリーズに収録されており、再版を重ねている。）

☆*Anne of Green Gables*（1908）『赤毛のアン』村岡花子訳，新潮文庫，1954.

☆*Anne of Avonlea*（1909）『アンの青春』村岡花子訳，新潮文庫，1955.

☆*Kilmeny of the Orchard*（1910）『果樹園のセレナーデ』村岡花子訳，新潮文庫，1961.

☆*The Story Girl*（1911）『ストーリー・ガール』木村由利子訳，篠崎書林，1980.

☆*Chronicles of Avonlea*（1912）『アンの友達』村岡花子訳，新潮文庫，1957.

☆*The Golden Road*（1913）『黄金の道』木村由利子訳，篠崎書林，1980.

☆*Anne of the Island*（1915）『アンの愛情』村岡花子訳，新潮文庫，1956.

☆*Anne's House of Dream*（1917）『アンの夢の家』村岡花子訳，新潮文庫，1958.

The Watchman and Other Poems（Toronto: McClelland. Goodchild, and Stewart, 1916）『夜警』吉川道夫・柴田恭子訳，篠崎書林，1986.

The Alpine Path（Everywomen's World 誌に連載 1917, Fitzhenry & Whiteside, 1974 ; Reprint: 1990）『険しい道──モンゴメリ自叙伝』山口昌子訳，篠崎書林，1979.

☆*Rainbow Valley*（1919）『虹の谷のアン』村岡花子訳，新潮文庫，1958.

☆*Rilla of Ingleside*（1921）『アンの娘リラ』村岡花子訳，新潮文庫，1959.

☆*Emily of New Moon*（1923）『可愛いエミリー』村岡花子訳，新潮文庫，1964.

☆*Emily Climbs*（1925）『エミリーはのぼる』村岡花子訳，新潮文庫，1967.

☆*The Blue Castle*（1926）『青い城』谷口由美子訳，篠崎書林，1983.

☆*Emily's Quest*（1927）『エミリーの求めるもの』村岡花子訳，新潮文庫，1969.

☆*Magic for Marigold*（1929）『マリーゴールドの魔法』田中とき子訳，篠崎書林、1983.

☆*A Tangled Web*（1931）『もつれた蜘蛛の巣』谷口由美子訳，篠崎書林，1983.

☆*Pat of Silver Bush*（1933）『銀の森のパット』田中とき子訳，篠崎書林，1980-81.

Courageous Women（共著 Toronto: McCleland and Stewart, 1934）

☆*Mistress Pat*（1935）『パットお嬢さん』村岡花子訳，新潮文庫，1965.

☆*Anne of Windy Poplars*（1936）『アンの幸福』村岡花子訳，新潮文庫，1958.

☆*Jane of Lantern Hill*（1937）『丘の家のジェーン』村岡花子訳，新潮文庫，1960.

☆*Anne of Ingleside*（1939）『炉辺荘のアン』村岡花子訳，新潮文庫，1958.

☆*Further Chronicles of Avonlea*（1920）『アンをめぐる人々』村岡花子訳，新潮文庫，1959.

The Road to Yesterday（ed. by Dr. Stuart Macdonald. Toronto: McGrow-Hill Ryerson, 1974）『アンの村の日々』上坪正徳訳，篠崎書林，1983.

　※『アン』シリーズは、「完訳クラッシック赤毛のアン」（講談社、1990-2000年）掛川恭子訳もある。

【2】日記

Rubio, Mary and Elizabeth Waterston, eds. *The Selected Journals of L.M. Montgomery*. Vol. 1〜5. Toronto: Oxford University press, 1985〜2004. 邦訳『モンゴメリ日記1〜3（1889〜1900）』桂宥子訳, 立風書房, 1995〜1997.

【3】書簡集

Eggleston, Wilfrid ed. *The Green Gables Letters from L.M. Montgomery to Ephraim Weber 1905-1909*. Toronto: Ryerson, 1960. Ottawa: Borealis Press, 1981.

Bolger, Francis W.P. and Elizabeth R. Epperly. *My dear Mr. M：Letters to G.B. Macmillan*. Toronto: McGraw-Hill Ryerson, 1980. 邦訳『モンゴメリ書簡集Ⅰ』宮武潤三・順子訳, 篠崎書林, 1981.

【4】伝記・評伝

Bolger, Francis W.P. *The Years Before 'Anne'*. Charlottetown, P.E.I.: Prince Edward Island Heritage Foundation, 1974.

Gillen, Mollie. *The Wheel of Things*. Halifax: Goodread Biographies, 1975. 邦訳『運命の紡ぎ車』宮武潤三・順子訳, 篠崎書林, 1979.

Bruce, Harry. *Maud*. New York: Bantam Books, 1992. 邦訳『モンゴメリ』橘 高弓枝訳, 偕成社, 1996.

Rubio, Mary and Elizabeth Waterston. *Writing a Life: L.M. Montgomery*. Toronto: BCW Press, 1995. 邦訳『〈赤毛のアン〉の素顔　L.M. モンゴメリ』槙朝子訳, ほるぷ出版, 1996.

McCabe, Kevin, Compiled & Alexandre Heilbron ed. *The Lucy Maud Montgomery Album*. Toronto: Fitzhenry & Shiteside, 1999.

The Bend in the Road. L.M. Montgomery Institute, 2000. http://www.upei.ca/〜lmmi/〈CD-ROM〉

梶原由佳『「赤毛のアン」を書きたくなかったモンゴメリ』青山出版, 2000.

【5】研究

Katsura, Yuko. 'Red-haird Anne in Japan.' *Canadian Children's Litrature*. No. 34, 1984.

Åhmansson, Gabriella. *A Life and Its Mirrors: A Feminist Reading of the Work of L.M. Montgomery*. Uppsala: University of Uppasala Press, 1991.

Epperly, Elizabeth Rollins. *The Fragrance of Sweet-Grass*. Toronto: University of Toronto Press, 1992.

横川寿美子『「赤毛のアンの挑戦」』宝島社, 1994.

Baldwin, Douglas. *Land of the Red Soil*. Charlottetown: Ragweed Press,1990. 邦訳『赤毛のアンの島』木村和男訳, 河出書房新社, 1995.

テリー神川『「赤毛のアン」の生活事典』講談社, 1997.

Barry, Wendy E., Margaret Anne Doody and Mary E. Doody Jones, eds. *The Annotated Anne of Green Gables*. New York: Oxford University Press, 1997. 邦訳『完全版　赤毛のアン』山本史郎訳, 原書房, 1999.

Gammel, Irene, and Elizabeth Epperly. *L.M. Montgomery and Canadian Culture*. Toronto: University of Toronto Press, 1999.

赤松佳子「少女の想像力、観察力、表現力──『赤毛のアン』」『英米児童文学ガイド』研究社出版, 2001.

索引

● あ ●

- アヴォンリー 48
- 『青い城』 67
- 『赤毛のアン』 4, 47
- 『赤毛のアンの手作り絵本』 82
- アトウッド，マーガレット 77
- 『アンデルセン童話集』 16
- アンドリューズ，プリシー 26
- 『アンの愛情』 61, 62
- 『アンの幸福』 70
- 『アンの青春』 53
- 『アンの友達』 60, 61
- 『アンの娘リラ』 61, 64
- 『アンの夢の家』 58, 61, 62, 69
- 『アンをめぐる人々』 68
- イブニング・メイル紙 34
- ヴァランシー 67
- ウィーバー，E 46
- ウィギン 76
- ウィル 24
- ウルナー，ルーシー 13
- 『運命の紡ぎ車』 5
- 『エミリーの求めるもの』 64
- 『エミリーはのぼる』 64
- 『L.M. モンゴメリとカナダ文化』 83
- 『黄金の道』 64
- 『丘の家のジェーン』 70
- 「おばけの森」 10
- オルコット 76
- 『オンディーヌ』 15

● か ●

- ガードナー，ロイヤル 62
- 「輝く湖水」 49
- 『果樹園のセレナーデ』 59
- カナダ連邦 8
- 『可愛いエミリー』 64
- キャヴェンディシュ 10, 48
- キャロル，ルイス 80
- ギルバート 49
- ギレン，M. 5

- 『銀の森のパット』 55, 68
- 「銀の森屋敷」 10
- グウェルフ大学 7
- クーリッジ 76
- クラークソン，エイドリエン 73
- 「グリーン・ゲイブルズ」 48
- クリフトン 12
- グレイ，ウォルター・T. 6
- グレー，ルーシー 15
- 『ケティが何をしたか』 76
- 『険しい道』 5, 64
- 「恋人の小径」 10, 48, 49
- 『ゴールデン・デイズ』 34

● さ ●

- 『サバイバル』 77
- シートン，アーネスト・T. 77
- シェイクスピア 16
- シャーリー，アン 48
- シャーロットタウン 8
- 『少女レベッカ』 76
- シンプソン，エド 35
- スコット 17
- スチュアート 61
- 『ストーリー・ガール』 59
- 『スペクテイター』 52
- 「スミレだけが」 18
- 「スミレの谷」 49

● た ●

- ダイアナ 62
- 「旅路の果て荘」 69
- 多文化主義 83
- ダルハウジー大学 34
- チェスター 61
- デイリー・エコー社 44
- テニソン 16, 34
- トウェイン，マーク 4

● な ●

- 『虹の谷のアン』 61, 63

索引

ニューロンドン ……………………………12
ノーヴァル ……………………………………66

● は ●

パーク・コーナー ……………………………35
ハーマン ………………………………………38
パイオニア紙 …………………………………43
バイロン …………………………………16, 34
『パットお嬢さん』 …………………………69
バラ ……………………………………………67
ハリファックス ………………………………33
ハワース ………………………………………59
『パンジー』 …………………………………24
ビディファンド ………………………………31
ヒュー …………………………………………61
フィリップス先生 ……………………………26
フーケ，モルト男爵 …………………………15
『不思議の国のアリス』 ……………………80
ブラウニング …………………………………16
フリード ………………………………………57
プリンス・アルバート …………………5, 13
プリンス・エドワード島 …………………7, 12
プリンス・オブ・ウエールズ・カレッジ …28
プリンスタウン ………………………………12
プロブレム・ノベル …………………………52
ペイジ社 …………………………………51, 69
ベデック，ロウア ……………………………37
ベルモント ……………………………………35
ヘンリー・ホルト社 …………………………50
ホイッティア ……………………………17, 34
ボブズ=メリル社 ……………………………50

● ま ●

マクシャノン，メアリー ……………………12
マクドナルド，ジョン・A. …………………21
マクドナルド，ユーアン ……………………53
マクニール，アレグザンダー ………………13
マクニール，ウィリアム・シンプソン ……12
マクニール，クレアラ・ウルナー …………12

マクミラン，G.B. ……………………………46
マクミラン社 …………………………………50
マシュー ………………………………………48
マスタード先生 ………………………………25
『マリーゴールドの魔法』 …………………68
マリラ …………………………………………48
「マルコポーロ号の遭難」 …………………18
村岡花子 ………………………………………81
「メルティング・ポット」 …………………83
モーリス，ケイティ …………………………15
「モザイク国家」 ……………………………83
『もつれた蜘蛛の巣』 ………………………67
モンゴメリ，ドナルド ………………………8
『モンゴメリ日記』 …………………………5
モンゴメリ，ヒュー …………………………12
モンゴメリ，ヒュー・ジョン ………………12
『モントリオール・ウィットネス』 ………17

● や ●

『夜警』 ………………………………………64
『ユース・コンパニオン』 …………………34

● ら ●

リースクデール ………………………………60
ルビオ，メアリー ……………………………5
レイチェル夫人 ………………………………49
『レッド・フォックス』 ……………………78
『レディーズ・ワールド』 …………………18
「レフォルス岬の伝説」 ……………………17
ロバーツ，チャールズ・G.D. ………………77
ロースロップ・リー・シェパード社 ………50
ローソン，メアリー …………………………18
ローラ …………………………………………24
ロングフェロー ………………………………34

● わ ●

ワーズワース …………………………………16
『若草物語』 …………………………………76
『悪い子の日記』 ……………………………6

■ あとがき ■

　この数年来、私は手作りの教材を使って学生たちと一緒に『赤毛のアン』とその作者L.M. モンゴメリについて学んできました。本書はその成果をまとめる絶好の機会となりました。

　本書の〈その生涯〉では、今や『赤毛のアン』とその作者の研究に欠かすことのできないモンゴメリの日記にもとづいて、人間味あふれるモンゴメリ像を浮き彫りにするよう努めました。そのハイライトは、何と言ってもモンゴメリの生い立ちが『赤毛のアン』の誕生とどのようにかかわったかという点でしょう。

　〈作品小論〉では、永遠の謎である『赤毛のアン』の人気の秘密を、いくつかの角度から探りました。

　〈作品鑑賞〉では、『赤毛のアン』の名場面の代表例として3章と15章の原文を引用しました。本書48頁の「ストーリー紹介」を参照すれば、名作『アン』の大まかな筋がわかるように編集しました。

　さらに、本書の魅力は、『モンゴメリ日記』の原文にも触れられる点でしょう。『日記』と『アン』の抜粋を比較しながら読むと、しばしば、自分の日記をそのまま、あるいはその中の子どもらしい発想を使うモンゴメリの創作方法を知ることができます。これは『赤毛のアン』の新たな作品理解に役立つことでしょう。

　コンパクトながらモンゴメリと『赤毛のアン』の情報が満載された本書をステップに、さらにモンゴメリとその作品に興味を持たれる読者がいれば、著者としてこの上ない喜びです。

桂　宥子

■ 著者紹介 ■　　桂　宥子（かつらゆうこ）

東京都出身。
立教大学大学院（英米文学）修了。
元トロント公共図書館「少年少女の家」司書。
現在、岡山県立大学教授。
著書
『アリス紀行』（東京図書）
『理想の児童図書館を求めて―トロントの「少年少女の家」』（中公新書）
『ジャンル・テーマ別英米児童文学』（共著，中教出版）
『はじめて学ぶ　英米児童文学史』（共編著，ミネルヴァ書房）
『英米児童文学の黄金時代』（共著，ミネルヴァ書房）ほか多数
訳書
『ちいさいケーブルカーのメーベル』（ペンギン社）
『人魚姫』（ほるぷ出版）
『赤毛のアンのクックブック』（東京図書）
『娘たちのマザーグース』『野生の一族』『モンゴメリ日記 / プリンス・エドワード島の少女』『モンゴメリ日記 / 十九歳の決心』『モンゴメリ日記 / 愛，その光と影』（立風書房）ほか多数

■ 写真協力 ■　　「口絵」「その生涯」オリオンプレス
「その生涯」立風書房（『モンゴメリ日記／プリンス・エドワード島の少女』）
「作品小論」赤毛のアン記念館・村岡花子文庫

■ 現代英米児童文学評伝叢書2 ■

L.M. モンゴメリ

2003年　4月10日　初版発行
2006年11月20日　初版第2刷発行

● 著　者 ●
桂　宥子

● 編　者 ●
谷本誠剛・原　昌・三宅興子・吉田新一

● 発行人 ●
前田哲次

● 発行所 ●
KTC中央出版

〒107-0062
東京都港区南青山6-1-6-201
TEL03-3406-4565

● 印刷 ●
凸版印刷株式会社

©Katsura Yuko
Printed in Japan　ISBN4-87758-264-9　C1398
乱丁、落丁本はお取り替えいたします。

刊行のことば

　日本イギリス児童文学会創設30周年にあたり、その記念事業の一つとして同学会編「現代英米児童文学評伝叢書」12巻を刊行することになりました。周知の通り英米児童文学はこれまで世界の児童文学の先導役を務めてきました。20世紀から現在まで活躍した作家たちのなかから、カナダを含め12人を精選し、ここにその＜人と生涯＞を明らかにし、作品小論を加え、原文の香りにも触れうるようにしました。

　これまでにこの種の類書はなく、はじめての英米児童文学の主要作家の評伝であり、児童文学を愛好するものにとって児童文学への関心がいっそう深まるよう、また研究を進めるものにとって基礎文献となるように編集されています。

日本イギリス児童文学会
　編集委員／谷本誠剛　　原　昌　　三宅興子　　吉田新一

◆現代英米児童文学評伝叢書◆

1	ローラ・インガルス・ワイルダー	磯部孝子
2	L.M. モンゴメリ	桂　宥子
3	エリナー・ファージョン	白井澄子
4	A.A. ミルン	谷本誠剛　笹田裕子
5	アーサー・ランサム	松下宏子
6	アリソン・アトリー	佐久間良子
7	J.R.R. トールキン	水井雅子
8	パメラ・L. トラヴァース	森　恵子
9	ロアルド・ダール	富田泰子
10	フィリッパ・ピアス	ピアス研究会
11	ロバート・ウェストール	三宅興子
12	E.L. カニグズバーグ	横田順子